Demon Trainer:

Exiled by Light, Forged in Flame

I0552988

"They called it a curse. She calls it training."

Copyright Page

Demon Trainer

First Edition: 2025

ISBN Paperback: 978-1-966703-18-1

ISBN eBook: 978-1-966703-19-8

Cover and interior design by Ken Konet

Printed in the United States of America

For more information about the author and upcoming works, visit: [Your website/social media to be added]

Table of Contents

Prologue: The Demon Who Waited

In a cavern of cooled fire beneath Calyss, Ashfang remembers when spirits were whole.

The darkness suited him just fine, thank you very much.

Ashfang stretched his claws against the obsidian floor of his prison—though "prison" was such an ugly word. The Council preferred "containment chamber" or "protective holding." As if slapping a pretty bow on a cage made it anything other than what it was.

Five hundred years of this. Five hundred years of listening to the city above him hum with life while he moldered in the deep places, forgotten except when someone needed a boogeyman for their bedtime stories.

He remembered when it wasn't like this. When spirits walked whole beneath sun and stars, neither light nor shadow but something richer—something complete. Before the Great Sundering tore them all in half like some cosmic toddler ripping apart a perfectly good toy.

Back then, we had names that meant something, he mused, tail flicking against the stone. *Now I'm just*

'demon.' Might as well call me 'Scary McFire-breath'
and be done with it.

The bitter irony wasn't lost on him. The Council had
split every spirit in two, branded half of them evil,
and then wondered why those halves grew sharp
edges in the dark. Centuries of rejection had a way
of teaching a fellow to bite first and ask questions
later. Hope, as it turned out, was a dangerous ember
to keep burning when all you got for your trouble
was another century of solitude.

But still, he kept it lit. That stubborn little flame of
maybe, someday, someone would call his name
without flinching.

Above him, the stones began to vibrate with familiar
rhythm. Naming Day. The one day a year when
sixteen-year-old humans played spiritual roulette,
stepping into those silver circles and calling out to
whatever might answer.

Usually, it was the light-halves who responded. The
Guardians with their pristine wings and noble
poses, ready to bond with some fresh-faced kid
who'd never known a day of real hardship. Perfect
matches for a perfect world built on perfectly
maintained lies.

Ashfang had stopped getting excited about Naming
Days around year two hundred. Hope was
exhausting when it never paid off.

But today... today felt different.

The chanting grew stronger, more desperate.
Someone up there was trying really, really hard to
prove they mattered. The kind of trying that came

from a place he recognized—the raw ache of wanting to belong somewhere, anywhere, even if it hurt.

Then he heard it. A voice cutting through the sacred words, unafraid and utterly alone:

"I call to the spirit who will have me. Any spirit. Please."

The summoning circle above flared ember-red, and for the first time in five centuries, Ashfang felt the pull. Not the casual tug of someone fishing for power, but the desperate grip of someone who needed him specifically. Someone who'd rather bond with a demon than remain empty.

He could have ignored it. Should have, probably. Nothing good ever came from answering that call.

But that voice...

Ashfang rose from his crouch, shadows wreathing around his horned skull like a crown made of midnight. His ember-eyes blazed as he felt the summoning take hold, felt the ancient magic reach down into his prison and offer him what he'd craved for half a millennium.

A chance.

As the world above reached for him and the stone around him began to crack, Ashfang allowed himself one last sardonic smile.

"Finally," he rumbled, and let the darkness carry him home.

Chapter 1: The Day of Naming

Kaela Veyne had exactly three minutes to decide if she was brave enough to potentially ruin her entire life.

She stood at the edge of Calyss's main square, watching her classmates step into the silver-and-salt circles like they were walking into their own personal fairy tales. Which, let's be honest, most of them were. Naming Day was supposed to be magical. It was supposed to be the moment when you discovered your Guardian spirit and officially became someone who mattered.

Supposed to being the key phrase here.

"Next!" called Elder Thorne, his voice carrying across the square with all the warmth of a tax collector. "Sera Brightwind!"

Sera—because of course her last name was Brightwind—practically floated into the circle. Her blonde hair caught the morning sun like spun gold, and her smile could have powered the city's street lamps for a week. Everything about her screamed 'destined for greatness,' which was deeply annoying on multiple levels.

Kaela watched from the crowd as Sera closed her eyes and began the traditional chant. The words were old, formal, and about as exciting as reading a grain inventory:

"By salt and silver, by blood and breath, I call to the spirit meant for me. Guardian of light, I offer my soul as vessel, my life as purpose. Come forth and be bound."

The silver circle flared with golden light so bright Kaela had to squint. When the glow faded, a magnificent wolf stood beside Sera—Solivane, the Dawn Wolf, whose coat seemed to contain actual sunbeams. The crowd erupted in appreciative murmurs.

Of course. Perfect girl gets perfect Guardian. The universe had a twisted sense of humor.

Elder Thorne smiled—a rare, thin expression of approval. "Sera Brightwind, bonded to Solivane of the Dawn Pack. A perfect bond, as befits a family so dedicated to the Council's unshakable order. May your partnership bring glory to Calyss."

Sera beamed and gave a little curtsy that somehow managed not to look ridiculous. Solivane's golden eyes surveyed the crowd with the kind of noble dignity that made Kaela want to throw something.

"Next! Kaela Veyne!"

And there it was. Her name, hanging in the air like a challenge.

Kaela's parents stood in the crowd, her mother gripping her father's arm so tightly her knuckles had

9

gone white. They'd been supportive, of course. Encouraging. But she'd caught them whispering late at night, voices tight with worry. What if she ended up Hollow? What if no spirit answered at all?

Honestly, Hollow would be fine. Hollow meant safe. Hollow meant she could learn a trade, maybe become a baker or a scribe, live a perfectly ordinary life where nobody expected her to save the world or lead a guild or marry into nobility.

But as she stepped toward the circle, Kaela realized she didn't want safe. She wanted to matter. She wanted to belong somewhere, to someone, even if it was messy and complicated and nothing like the fairy tale everyone else seemed to be living.

The salt-and-silver circle felt cold beneath her bare feet. Elder Thorne gestured for her to begin, his expression already settling into the neutral mask he wore for the disappointments.

Kaela closed her eyes and tried to summon the same confidence Sera had radiated. She was going to do this. She was going to call a Guardian, and it was going to be magnificent, and everyone would finally see that she was more than just average.

"By salt and silver, by blood and breath..."

The words felt clumsy in her mouth, like she was speaking a language she'd only read in books. But she pushed forward, pouring every ounce of desperate hope into the ancient phrases.

"I call to the spirit meant for me. Guardian of light, I offer my soul as vessel, my life as purpose. Come forth and be bound."

Nothing happened.

The circle remained stubbornly silver. No golden glow. No majestic creature materializing to pledge eternal partnership. Just Kaela, standing alone in a ring of metal and salt while the crowd began to shift restlessly.

Elder Thorne cleared his throat. "Perhaps if you tried again, child. Sometimes the first attempt—"

"No." The word came out sharper than Kaela intended. She wasn't done. She wasn't giving up. Not when this was her one chance to prove she belonged in this world.

She threw the traditional words out the window and spoke from her heart instead:

"I call to the spirit who will have me. Any spirit. Please."

The circle exploded into ember-red flame.

This wasn't the warm golden glow of a Guardian bond. This was wild, chaotic, and hot enough to make the crowd step back in alarm. The fire twisted upward like a miniature tornado, and through it, Kaela heard something that made her blood run cold:

Laughter. Low, sardonic, and definitely not coming from anything that belonged in a children's bedtime story.

The flames parted like curtains, and Ashfang stepped through.

He was magnificent in the worst possible way. Twice the size of Solivane, with obsidian scales that seemed to drink the light around him. His horned skull tilted at an angle that suggested he found this entire situation deeply amusing, and his ember-bright eyes fixed on Kaela with something that might have been approval.

"Well," he said, voice like gravel mixed with smoke, "this is awkward."

The bond hit her like a lightning strike. Not the gentle warmth she'd expected from a Guardian connection, but something fierce and immediate that burned through her veins and settled in her chest like a second heartbeat. She could feel his amusement, his centuries of loneliness, his razor-sharp intelligence wrapped in layers of protective sarcasm.

He was hers. She was his. And absolutely everything was about to go sideways.

"Demon!" Elder Thorne's voice cracked like a whip. "A corruption of the sacred rite! You defy the wisdom of our founders and the purity they established!"

But it was too late. The bond had already sealed itself, wrapping around Kaela's soul like chains made of starlight and shadow. There was no undoing this. Whatever came next, she and Ashfang were in it together.

The crowd recoiled as if she'd sprouted a second head. Her parents stood frozen, love and law warring across their faces. Sera and her perfect wolf had backed away, golden eyes wide with something that looked suspiciously like fear.

Kaela looked at Ashfang—her demon, her partner, her completely catastrophic mistake—and felt a smile tug at the corners of her mouth.

"So," she said, surprised by how steady her voice sounded. "What happens now?"

Ashfang's grin revealed teeth like obsidian daggers. "Now, little fire-starter, we find out what you're really made of."

Chapter 2: The Demon Awakens

The containment chamber was exactly as welcoming as it sounded.

Kaela sat on a stone bench that had clearly been designed by someone who believed comfort was a character flaw, staring at the thick iron bars that separated her from the rest of the world. The walls were covered in glowing runes that made her skin itch, and the air tasted like copper pennies and regret.

Ashfang lounged in the corner like he owned the place, which was probably the most irritating thing about this entire situation. His obsidian scales caught the runelight and threw it back in patterns that hurt to look at directly. Every few minutes, his tail would flick against the stone floor with a sound like knives being sharpened.

"Stop doing that," Kaela muttered.

"Doing what?" His voice carried that same sardonic amusement from the square, like he was enjoying a private joke at the universe's expense.

"Being so... calm about this." She gestured at the bars, the runes, the general atmosphere of impending doom. "We're in prison."

"Ah." Ashfang's ember eyes fixed on her with the intensity of a predator sizing up prey. "And here I thought we were in a cozy little reading nook. My mistake."

The bond between them hummed with his amusement, and Kaela felt her own irritation spike in response. Which apparently was hilarious to him, because his mental chuckle echoed through her head like smoke.

"This isn't funny," she snapped.

"Isn't it?" He shifted position, and suddenly he seemed twice as large as before. "You called for any spirit that would have you. I answered. Now you're having second thoughts because I don't come with a golden mane and a superiority complex?"

"I didn't know—"

"That I was a demon? That bonding with me would make you a pariah? That your perfect little life was about to get thoroughly torched?" His voice dropped to something dangerously soft. "Or did you think you could somehow cheat the system? Get power without consequences?"

The words hit like physical blows, mostly because they were uncomfortably close to the truth. Kaela had wanted to matter, wanted to belong, but she'd never seriously considered what would happen if she got her wish in the worst possible way.

"I'm not a coward," she said, though her voice shook slightly.

"Prove it."

Before she could ask what he meant, the chamber door clanged open. Elder Thorne entered, flanked by two Guardians whose spirits—a crystal stag and an ember hawk—radiated disapproval so thick you could have cut it with a blade.

"Kaela Veyne," Elder Thorne intoned, "you stand accused of willful corruption and trafficking with forbidden spirits."

"Trafficking?" Kaela stood up, outrage overriding fear. "I didn't traffic with anyone! I called for a Guardian and got—"

"A demon." The word dripped from Thorne's mouth like poison. "A creature of shadow and malice that has no place among civilized people."

Ashfang yawned, showing off those obsidian-dagger teeth. "Charmed, I'm sure."

Thorne ignored him completely, which struck Kaela as both rude and strategically stupid.

"However, the Council recognizes that you may have been... misguided rather than malicious. Councilor Mirren himself has authorized this act of compassion. We are prepared to offer mercy."

He produced a crystal rod covered in silver runes that made Kaela's skin crawl just looking at it. The thing radiated wrongness, like the magical equivalent of nails on a chalkboard.

"A sealing rod," Thorne explained. "It will sever the corrupt bond and free you from this creature's influence. You'll be Hollow, but you'll be clean."

"And him?" Kaela asked, though she was pretty sure she didn't want to know the answer.

"The demon will be returned to its proper place. Contained. Forgotten."

The casual cruelty of it made Kaela's chest burn with something that felt suspiciously like protective fury. Through the bond, she felt Ashfang's surprise—and then his quick attempt to hide it behind mental walls.

Elder Thorne raised the sealing rod, and the runes along its length flared to life. "Hold still, child. This may feel uncomfortable, but—"

The rod exploded.

Not literally—that would have been too simple. Instead, the silver runes cracked and went dark, and the crystal itself turned the color of old blood before crumbling to ash in Thorne's hands.

"What—" Thorne stared at the remains of his fancy demon-severing stick like it had personally betrayed him.

"Oops," Ashfang said mildly. "Did I do that?"

But Kaela had felt what really happened. In the split second before the rod had tried to cut their bond, Ashfang had wrapped himself around her soul like a shield, taking the brunt of the severance attempt. The feedback had fried the crystal, but it had also left him looking slightly less solid around the edges. For a moment, his form seemed to flicker at the edges, like a flame starved of air. The effort had cost him, a visible drain on the very substance that held him together.

He'd protected her. At his own expense.

"You—" She started to thank him, but he cut her off with a mental snarl.

Don't. I need you functional if we're going to survive this mess.

Right. Purely practical. Nothing emotional about it at all.

Elder Thorne was conferring with his Guardian-bonded guards in urgent whispers. Finally, he turned back to Kaela with an expression that could have curdled milk.

"Very well. If you refuse purification, then you have chosen chaos over the sacred order our founders established. You leave us no choice." His voice carried across the chamber with formal finality. "By order of the Council of Light, Kaela Veyne is declared corrupted beyond redemption. At dawn, you will be exiled from Calyss and all civilized lands. Your parents have been notified."

Kaela's world tilted sideways. "You can't—I'm sixteen! You can't just throw me out to die!"

"We are not throwing you out to die," Thorne said with the kind of bureaucratic precision that suggested he'd given this speech before. "We are removing a dangerous influence from our community. What happens to you beyond our walls is between you and whatever darkness you've chosen to embrace."

He turned and strode from the chamber, his guards falling into step behind him. The door slammed shut with a finality that echoed in Kaela's bones.

"Well," Ashfang said after the echoes faded. "That went about as well as expected."

Kaela slumped back onto the stone bench, the full weight of her situation finally hitting her. Exiled. Cast out. Everything she'd ever known, everyone she'd ever loved, gone because she'd made one desperate choice in a moment of panic.

"I'm sorry," she whispered.

"For what?"

"For dragging you into this. For getting us both trapped. For—"

"For calling me?"

She looked up at him, expecting mockery, but his ember eyes were surprisingly gentle.

"You called," he said simply. "For five hundred years, I waited in the dark for someone to call my name without flinching. You didn't even know my name, but you called anyway." He shifted closer, and she could feel the warmth radiating from his scales. "Do you have any idea how long it's been since someone chose me? Not settled for me, not got stuck with me by accident, but actually chose?"

"But now we're both—"

"Free," he finished. "For the first time in centuries, I'm free. And tomorrow, when they open those gates and shove us into the Wilds, we'll figure out what that means."

Kaela wanted to argue, to point out that exile wasn't exactly freedom, but the conviction in his voice stopped her. Through their bond, she could feel something she hadn't expected: hope. Cautious, carefully guarded, but real.

As the hours crawled toward dawn, Kaela dozed fitfully on the stone bench. Just before sleep finally claimed her, she heard Ashfang's voice in her mind, softer than she'd ever heard it:

You lived. That matters.

And for the first time since the bonding, Kaela thought he might be right.

Chapter 3: Exile to the Wilds

The outer gate of Calyss opened with all the ceremony of a larder door.

No speeches. No final words of wisdom. Just two guards who couldn't quite meet Kaela's eyes as they gestured for her to step through the iron archway that separated civilization from whatever lay beyond. One of them—she thought his name was Marcus— had taught her basic swordwork in the youth corps. He'd smiled at her then, called her "quick on her feet" and "promising."

Now he looked at her like she was carrying plague.

Now he looked at her like she was carrying plague. Before shoving a canvas pack into her hands, he hesitated, his gaze darting toward the treeline.

"Best keep moving, Kaela," Marcus muttered, his voice barely a whisper. "The Hunters patrol these woods, and they don't show mercy to the corrupted." He then pushed the pack at her without making skin contact. "Your parents left this."

Kaela's throat tightened as she recognized her mother's careful stitching on the pack's straps. Inside, she found dried fruit, hard cheese, a water skin, a spare cloak, and a folded piece of paper covered in her father's precise handwriting:

We love you. We will always love you. Come home when you can.

The guards stepped back as Ashfang materialized beside her—apparently he could vanish and reappear at will, which was either very convenient or deeply unsettling. Probably both.

"Touching," he commented, reading over her shoulder with the casual boundary violations of someone who'd spent centuries alone. "Though 'come home when you can' assumes there will be a 'when you can' and not a 'when the wild hounds finish picking your bones clean.'"

"You're really bad at pep talks," Kaela said, tucking the note away carefully.

"I prefer to think of it as managing expectations."

The gate slammed shut behind them with a finality that made Kaela's stomach drop. She was outside. Actually, properly outside the walls for the first time in her life. The Wilds stretched ahead of them— rolling hills covered in twisted trees that looked like they'd been shaped by nightmares, fog-filled valleys that seemed to swallow sound, and in the distance, mountains that scraped the belly of storm clouds.

It was beautiful in the way that poisonous flowers were beautiful: lovely to look at, likely to kill you if you got too close.

"So," Kaela said, shouldering her pack and trying to project confidence she absolutely didn't feel. "Which way to the nearest inn?"

Ashfang's laugh sounded like gravel sliding down a mountain. "Oh, sweet summer child. The nearest 'inn' is about three days' walk through territory controlled by things that consider humans a delicacy. But please, lead the way."

Six hours later, Kaela was beginning to understand why exile was considered a death sentence.

Her feet hurt. Her stomach was performing an increasingly dramatic interpretation of 'empty.' Her spare cloak was soaked through from the persistent drizzle that had started the moment they'd left sight of the city walls. And somewhere in the fog-shrouded trees around them, things kept making sounds that definitely didn't come from any animal she'd learned about in natural philosophy class.

"Are you planning to actually help," she asked through chattering teeth, "or are you just going to follow me around making sarcastic commentary until I die of exposure?"

Ashfang, who hadn't shown the slightest sign of discomfort despite the cold and wet, tilted his horned head thoughtfully. "Well, the sarcastic commentary is one of my best features. But I suppose I could contribute to the 'not dying' effort."

He vanished into the shadows between the trees, leaving Kaela alone with the increasingly ominous forest sounds. For a moment, panic clawed at her throat—what if he'd abandoned her? What if the bond meant nothing to him and he'd simply been waiting for a chance to escape?

Then she heard something that made her blood freeze: the low, hunting howl of wild hounds.

They emerged from the fog like nightmares given form—six of them, each the size of a small horse, with matted fur and eyes that glowed sickly yellow in the dim light. Their teeth were too long, too sharp, and they moved with the coordinated precision of a pack that had brought down prey much larger than one teenage girl.

Kaela fumbled for the eating knife in her pack, knowing it was pathetically inadequate but needing something solid in her hands. The lead hound crouched, muscles bunching for a leap that would probably take her head clean off.

That's when Ashfang dropped out of the canopy like a falling star made of claws and fury.

He landed on the lead hound's back, obsidian talons raking deep furrows along its flanks. The creature howled—not in hunting triumph now, but in pain and rage. The rest of the pack scattered for a heartbeat, then regrouped, circling the new threat.

"Left flank!" Ashfang's voice cut through the chaos. "Two coming around!"

Kaela spun, saw the hounds trying to flank them, and did something that surprised her: she listened to the bond. There was something there, a sense of rightness, of partnership. She dropped low as one hound leaped over her head, then rolled aside as the second snapped at where she'd been.

Fire bloomed in her palms—not the wild, uncontrolled flame from the naming circle, but something focused, deliberate. She thrust both hands forward and sent a gout of flame into the nearest hound's face. It yelped and stumbled backward, singed and blinded.

"Nice!" Ashfang called, crushing another hound's leg with his jaws. "Again!"

For maybe ten seconds, they were perfect. Kaela provided fire support while Ashfang tore through the pack with surgical precision, their movements synchronized through the bond like they'd been practicing for years instead of hours.

Then it was over. The surviving hounds melted back into the fog, deciding that easier prey was probably available elsewhere.

Kaela stood in the sudden silence, hands still flickering with residual flames, staring at Ashfang. There was blood on his obsidian scales—not his own—and his ember eyes were bright with something that looked suspiciously like pride.

"Not bad for a first fight," he said. "Though your footwork needs improvement."

The adrenaline crashed out of Kaela's system all at once, leaving her shaky and nauseous. The reality of what had just happened hit her like a physical blow. She'd killed things. Burned them. And she'd enjoyed it.

"I can't do this," she whispered. "I can't be this person."

She turned and ran.

The bond stretched between them like a chain made of fire and shadow, and with every step she took away from Ashfang, it pulled tighter. By the time she'd made it a hundred yards through the twisted trees, the pain was excruciating. By two hundred yards, it felt like someone was slowly pulling her soul out through her ribs.

She collapsed behind a moss-covered boulder, gasping and clutching at her chest. Through the bond, she could feel Ashfang's exasperation, his concern, and underneath it all, something that felt like hurt.

You can run, his voice echoed in her mind, *but we're linked now. Permanently. You go too far, we both suffer.*

"I didn't ask for this," she said to the empty forest.

Neither did I. But here we are.

She heard his footsteps before she saw him—deliberate, unhurried, giving her time to compose herself. When he finally appeared around the boulder, he'd shrunk himself down to roughly human size, though he still looked like he could bite through steel.

"Better?" he asked.

Kaela wiped her eyes, hoping the dampness could be blamed on the persistent drizzle. "The pain stopped."

"It will, as long as we stay within a reasonable distance of each other. Think of it as cosmic encouragement to work out our issues."

They stared at each other across the small clearing. Kaela could feel his patience through the bond—not infinite, but deeper than she'd expected. Like he was willing to wait for her to figure this out, as long as she was actually trying.

"I've never killed anything before," she said finally.

"And now you have. How do you feel about it?"

"Terrible. Sick. Like I'm becoming something I don't recognize."

Ashfang considered this. "Those hounds would have torn you apart and left the pieces for scavengers. Your parents would have buried an empty coffin. I would have spent the next few centuries trapped in whatever passed for your corpse, slowly going insane from isolation." He tilted his head. "Still feel terrible about defending yourself?"

When he put it like that, it sounded almost reasonable. But Kaela wasn't ready to let go of her horror quite yet. "You enjoyed it. The fighting."

"I enjoyed the teamwork," he corrected. "For ten seconds, we moved like partners instead of strangers handcuffed together. It was... nice."

The admission caught her off guard. Through the bond, she could feel his sincerity, his cautious hope that maybe this partnership could be more than just mutual survival.

"I don't know how to do this," she said. "I don't know how to be someone who fights and kills and burns things."

27

"Then we'll figure it out together." Ashfang settled onto his haunches, making himself less imposing. "But first, we need shelter and food, or the philosophical questions become moot."

As if summoned by his words, Kaela's stomach released a growl that could probably be heard in the next valley. Despite everything, she found herself smiling.

"You mentioned hunting earlier."

"I did. Though I should probably warn you that my hunting style tends toward the 'thoroughly cooked' end of the spectrum."

"As long as it's edible."

"Oh, it will be. I have excellent taste in charred meat."

They made camp in a dry cave Ashfang found with his apparently supernatural nose for comfortable hiding spots. He disappeared for an hour and returned with something that might have been a deer, if deer grew to the size of small carriages and had too many teeth.

"Wild elk," he explained, settling the carcass down with the casual air of someone delivering groceries. "Aggressive, territorial, and absolutely delicious when properly prepared."

"Properly prepared meaning 'burned to a crisp'?"

"There are subtleties to flame-cooking that you clearly don't appreciate."

Kaela watched him methodically roast chunks of elk meat over flames that danced between his claws like trained pets. The smell was incredible—smoky and rich and nothing like the careful, civilized meals she'd grown up with.

"Ground rules," she said as they settled in to eat. "If we're stuck together, we need to establish some boundaries."

"Agreed. I'll start: no attempting to run away in the middle of fights. It's tactically unsound and gives me indigestion."

"Fine. And you don't get to make unilateral decisions about our survival. We're partners, not owner and pet."

"Fair enough. Though I reserve the right to override your suggestions if they're likely to get us both killed."

"And no roasting me if I do something stupid."

Ashfang's grin showed far too many teeth. "Define 'roasting.'"

"Actual fire. Applied to my person. With intent to cause harm."

"Agreed. What about sarcastic commentary regarding your poor life choices?"

"That seems to be essential to your personality, so I guess I'll have to live with it."

"Excellent. Any other demands?"

Kaela thought about it as she bit into the elk meat. It was, despite everything, absolutely delicious. "Just one. No matter how bad things get, we don't give up on each other. We're all we've got now."

Something shifted in Ashfang's ember eyes— surprise, maybe, or gratitude. "Agreed," he said softly. "No giving up."

They ate in companionable silence as night fell around their small cave. Outside, the Wilds hummed with dangerous life, but for the first time since the naming ceremony, Kaela felt like she might actually survive this.

As she drifted off to sleep, wrapped in her spare cloak and warmed by the heat radiating from Ashfang's scales, she heard him murmur:

"Not bad for a first day of exile."

And despite everything, she found herself smiling in the dark.

Chapter 4: Training Attempt #1

Three days of stumbling through the Wilds had taught Kaela exactly one thing: she was terrible at being exiled.

Her feet were a collection of blisters held together by stubborn pride. Her hair looked like she'd been wrestling with a particularly vindictive shrub (which, to be fair, she had—twice). And every time she tried to do something useful with her fire, it either fizzled out pathetically or nearly burned down whatever unfortunate vegetation happened to be nearby.

"This is ridiculous," she announced, glaring at the smoldering remains of what used to be a perfectly innocent berry bush. "I bonded with a demon. I should be powerful. I should be able to do more than accidentally commit arson."

Ashfang, who had been lounging in a patch of sunlight like the world's most dangerous cat, opened one ember eye. "Should be, could be, might be. Such inspiring words. I'm sure the next bush will be properly intimidated."

"I'm serious!" Kaela kicked at a rock, which accomplished nothing except making her toe hurt. "That fight with the hounds—for ten seconds, I felt like I knew what I was doing. Like the fire was actually listening to me instead of just doing whatever it wanted."

"And now you want to skip straight to the advanced course." Ashfang stretched, unfolding from his relaxed pose with liquid grace. "Tell me, when you learned to walk, did you start with running marathons?"

"Walking doesn't have the potential to incinerate half a forest."

"Fair point. Though I notice you're still standing, and the forest is only mostly singed. Progress!"

Kaela wanted to argue, but the bond carried too much genuine amusement for her to stay properly annoyed. "You're enjoying this."

"I'm enjoying watching someone discover that power isn't just about wanting it hard enough. It's refreshing, honestly. Most humans seem to think bonding with a spirit is like buying a sword—pay the price, swing it around, instant results."

"So what's the secret? How do I actually use this thing?" She gestured vaguely at the space between them, where their bond hummed with potential energy.

Ashfang's expression grew thoughtful. "Show me everything you've got."

"What?"

"Full power. No holding back. Let me see what we're working with."

Kaela blinked. "Are you sure? Because the last time I tried that, I nearly took Elder Thorne's eyebrows off."

"I'm not Elder Thorne. And unlike him, I'm actually fireproof." Ashfang's grin showed those obsidian-dagger teeth. "Besides, how bad could it be?"

Famous last words.

Kaela closed her eyes and reached for the fire inside her chest. Not the careful, controlled flame she'd been trying to manage, but the wild, chaotic heat that had erupted during the naming ceremony. She grabbed hold of it with both hands and pulled.

The world exploded into crimson light.

Fire roared out of her in every direction—not the focused gouts she'd been attempting, but a spherical wave of superheated air that turned every piece of vegetation within thirty feet into instant kindling. The blast was so intense that rocks cracked from thermal shock, and somewhere in the distance, she was pretty sure she heard a tree fall over.

When the flames finally died down, Kaela found herself standing in the center of a perfectly circular patch of ash and charcoal. Her cloak was smoking. Her eyebrows were definitely shorter than they'd been a minute ago. And the air tasted like burned everything.

"Well," Ashfang said from somewhere behind her, voice carefully neutral. "That was certainly... comprehensive."

Kaela turned to find him wreathed in shadows so thick they looked almost solid. The darkness had formed a protective shell around him, deflecting the worst of her fireburst. But even through his supernatural defenses, she could see singed patches on his scales.

"Oh no. Oh no, I'm so sorry, I didn't mean to—"

"Kaela." His voice cut through her panic with surprising gentleness. "Breathe."

She tried, but her lungs felt like they were full of hot sand. The fire inside her chest was still raging, still demanding release, and she could feel it building toward another explosion.

"I can't—it won't stop—"

Ashfang's shadows flowed toward her like living smoke, wrapping around her shoulders and arms with cool, soothing pressure. The contrast between her internal fire and his external darkness was so stark it made her gasp, but the flames finally began to settle.

"There," he murmured. "Shadow and flame. They balance each other, if you let them."

Kaela sagged against him, suddenly consumed by a profound spiritual exhaustion. It was a hollowness that went deeper than muscle fatigue, a bone-deep chill as if she had burned away a part of her own essence to fuel the inferno.

Through their bond, she could feel his concern, his quiet strength, and underneath it all, something that felt like pride.

"That was terrible," she whispered. "I could have killed you. I could have killed us both."

"But you didn't." Ashfang's voice rumbled through his chest, a sound like distant thunder. "You held it together long enough for me to help. That's not nothing."

"It's not enough, either." Kaela pulled back to look at him, taking in the singed patches on his scales, the careful way he was holding his left wing. "I hurt you."

"Barely. And only because I wasn't expecting quite that much enthusiasm." His ember eyes met hers. "Why?"

"Why what?"

"Why does it matter so much? The power, the control, the need to prove yourself?" His head tilted in that considering way of his. "What are you really trying to accomplish here?"

Kaela wanted to deflect, to make a joke or change the subject. But something in his expression stopped her. He wasn't mocking her or pushing for entertainment. He genuinely wanted to understand.

"I spent my whole life being average," she said finally. "Average grades, average skills, average everything. My parents love me, but they never expected much. My teachers were polite but not particularly interested. When Sera summoned Solivane, everyone acted like it was inevitable—of course the perfect girl gets the perfect Guardian."

She kicked at the ash around her feet. "But when I called for you, for the first time in my life, something extraordinary happened. Something that mattered. And I guess I thought..." She trailed off, embarrassed by her own desperation.

"You thought bonding with a demon would automatically make you special," Ashfang finished, not unkindly.

"Sounds pretty stupid when you say it like that."

"Not stupid. Human." He settled onto his haunches, bringing his eyes level with hers. "But here's the thing about being special—it's not about the power you can channel or the spirit you're bonded to. It's about what you choose to do with whatever you've got."

Kaela studied his face, looking for signs of the sarcasm she'd grown used to. But his expression was surprisingly serious.

"You think I'm choosing wrong?"

"I think you're trying to sprint before you've learned to walk. And in our case, falling down doesn't just mean scraped knees." He gestured at the circle of devastation around them. "It means accidentally turning forests into bonfires and partners into charcoal."

The criticism stung, mostly because it was accurate. "So what do you suggest?"

"Start at the beginning. Breath, stance, focus. Learn to feel the fire before you try to direct it." Ashfang's grin returned, edged with challenge. "And maybe work on naming what you're actually afraid of."

"I'm not afraid—"

"Everyone's afraid of something. Fear is fuel, if you know how to use it. But if you pretend it doesn't exist, it'll burn you from the inside out."

Kaela wanted to argue, but the words died in her throat. Because the truth was, she was afraid. Terrified, actually. Afraid of being ordinary, afraid of failing, afraid of discovering that even with a demon bond, she still wasn't good enough to matter.

"I'm afraid of being forgotten," she admitted quietly. "Of living my whole life without leaving a mark on anything."

"There we go." Ashfang's voice carried approval and something that might have been understanding. "That's honest. That's something we can work with."

"How?"

"Fire feeds on emotion—fear, anger, joy, grief. But it needs direction, or it just burns everything equally." He shifted position, scales catching the afternoon light. "The next time you reach for your flame, don't try to prove anything. Just breathe, feel what you're feeling, and name it. Then ask the fire to help instead of demanding it obey."

It sounded simple. Which probably meant it was going to be anything but.

"And if I accidentally torch another forest?"

"Then we'll find a new forest. The Wilds are full of them." Ashfang's expression softened slightly. "But I don't think you will. You held back with the hounds when you needed to, and you pulled back just now when I asked. You've got the instincts, Kaela. You just need to trust them."

They spent the rest of the afternoon working on what Ashfang called "the fundamentals." Breathing exercises that synced her heartbeat with the rhythm of flames. Stance work that helped her feel grounded and stable. And most importantly, the practice of naming her emotions before trying to channel them.

It was frustrating, tedious work. Instead of dramatic fireballs, she produced steady candle flames. Instead of spectacular displays of power, she learned to light kindling without burning down the surrounding area.

But as the sun set and they settled around their small, carefully controlled campfire, Kaela felt something she hadn't expected: satisfaction. Not the desperate need to prove herself, but the quiet pleasure of actually understanding something new.

"Better?" Ashfang asked, noting her expression.

"Different," Kaela said. "It doesn't feel as... urgent."

"Good. Urgent leads to mistakes. And in our line of work, mistakes tend to be explosive."

They ate their dinner—more of Ashfang's expertly charred meat—in comfortable silence. The Wilds hummed around them with their usual collection of ominous sounds, but somehow they seemed less threatening now. Maybe because Kaela was starting to understand that she didn't have to face them alone.

"Thank you," she said as they banked the fire for the night.

"For what?"

"For not giving up on me. For being patient when I was being an idiot about power and control."

Ashfang's chuckle rumbled through the bond. "Oh, you're still going to be an idiot about plenty of things. But we'll figure it out as we go."

"Encouraging as always."

"I prefer 'realistic.' But if it helps, you're already better than you were this morning. Tomorrow, you'll be better than you are tonight. That's how improvement works—one small step at a time."

As Kaela drifted off to sleep, she found herself thinking about those words. One small step at a time. It wasn't the dramatic transformation she'd been hoping for, but maybe that was okay. Maybe being extraordinary didn't have to happen all at once.

Maybe it could happen one breath at a time.

Chapter 5: Hunters Close In

The thing about being hunted, Kaela discovered, was that it made everything else seem remarkably unimportant.

She crouched behind a moss-covered boulder, trying to keep her breathing steady while her heart attempted to beat its way out of her chest.

Fifty yards away, through the morning mist, she could see them: three Council Hunters and their Guardian spirits. Their armor was polished steel, etched with runes of protection that pulsed with a faint golden light, a stark contrast to the mottled leather of the exiles. They moved without words, communicating through hand signals with the silent efficiency of a well-oiled machine.

A lot.

"How long have they been tracking us?" she whispered to Ashfang, who had flattened himself against the stone beside her, scales shifting color to match the granite.

"Since yesterday, probably." His mental voice carried grim satisfaction. "I was wondering when they'd catch up. Three days is actually longer than I expected—you're getting better at covering your tracks."

"Is that supposed to be comforting?"

"Would you prefer I lie and tell you we're perfectly safe?"

Before Kaela could answer, a harsh cry echoed through the forest. Above them, a red-gold hawk circled on thermal currents, ember eyes scanning the ground below with predatory focus.

"Pyrris," Ashfang identified, pressing lower against the rock. "Tracking spirit. And where there's a Pyrris..."

Stone erupted from the forest floor in a series of sharp ridges, blocking the deer path they'd been following and sealing off the narrow valley behind them. The earth groaned and shifted as more barriers rose, systematically cutting off every escape route Kaela could see.

"Calior," she breathed, recognizing the massive crystal stag from her lessons on Guardian spirits. "Stone manipulation. They're herding us." The hawk cried out again, and the stag responded instantly, raising another wall of earth. They were a unit, human and spirit working as extensions of the Council's will.

"Into a very obvious trap, yes. The question is whether we spring it or find a more creative solution." Ashfang's ember eyes fixed on her. "How's your spark-scatter coming along?"

Kaela flexed her fingers, feeling the familiar tingle of flame waiting just beneath her skin. They'd been practicing the technique for two days—small, rapid bursts of fire designed to confuse rather than destroy. It was delicate work, requiring the kind of precise control she was still learning.

"Better than my forest-torching, worse than my lighting-campfires."

"Good enough. When I give the signal, I want you to fill the air between us and them with as much chaos as you can manage. Don't aim to hit anything—just make it impossible for them to see clearly."

"What are you going to do?"

Ashfang's grin was all teeth and dark promise. "Something spectacular and probably stupid."

The Hunters had spread out in a standard search pattern, their Guardian spirits providing overlapping coverage of the area. Kaela recognized the formation from her tactical studies—designed to flush prey into the open where superior numbers and firepower could end things quickly.

Unfortunately for them, neither she nor Ashfang were particularly interested in playing the role of prey.

"Now," Ashfang whispered.

He exploded from cover like a shadow given violent life, charging straight at the center of their formation with a roar that made the trees shake. It was exactly the kind of frontal assault that any sensible person would avoid—which was probably why it worked.

The Hunters scrambled to respond, their Guardian spirits wheeling to face this new threat. Calior's antlers began to glow as he prepared another stone barrier, while Pyrris dove from above with talons extended.

That's when Kaela stood up and turned the morning mist into a lightshow.

Fire bloomed from her hands in dozens of small, brilliant bursts—not the overwhelming explosion she'd produced during training, but a rapid-fire barrage of sparks that filled the air like angry stars. Each burst was perfectly controlled, lasting just long enough to blind before winking out and being replaced by another.

The effect was exactly what Ashfang had hoped for: instant chaos. The Hunters couldn't see their target, couldn't coordinate their attacks, couldn't even tell where the fire was coming from. Pyrris, diving blind through the sparks, missed Ashfang entirely and crashed into a tree trunk with an undignified squawk.

"Left!" Ashfang's voice cut through the confusion. "Guardian duelist with a sealing spear!"

Kaela spun, saw the Hunter emerging from behind Calior's stone barrier, and adjusted her spark pattern to keep him blinded. The man was older than the others, moving with the kind of fluid grace that spoke of decades of training. His uniform bore the silver chevrons of a senior Hunter, and the crystal-tipped spear in his hands hummed with containment runes.

He couldn't see clearly, but he didn't need to. He'd done this enough times to know where a demon-bonded exile would be standing, and his spear thrust was aimed with professional precision at the space where Ashfang should have been.

Should have been, but wasn't. Because Ashfang had already moved, flowing like liquid shadow around the stone barriers, putting Calior between himself and the spear-wielding Hunter.

But the Hunter had anticipated that too. As Ashfang rounded the crystalline stag, the man reversed his grip and swept the spear in a wide arc, not trying to kill but to graze, to make contact with the runes that would suppress Ashfang's abilities.

The crystal tip caught Ashfang along his left ribs, leaving a thin line of silver fire across his obsidian scales.

The effect was immediate and terrifying. Ashfang's roar cut off mid-note as the containment magic took hold, and Kaela felt something awful happen to their bond—like someone had wrapped chains around a vital organ and started pulling tight.

Through their connection, she felt the numbness creeping up Ashfang's side, deadening his natural fire resistance and making his movements sluggish. The runes were designed to suppress demonic abilities, to make spirits docile and manageable.

Which meant they'd made a serious tactical error in underestimating what Kaela could do on her own.

Rage flooded through her—not the wild, uncontrolled fury she'd struggled with before, but something focused and purposeful. They were trying to cage her partner, to reduce him to a shadow of himself. That was unacceptable.

"Ashfang!" she called. "Smoke screen!"

He understood immediately. Even weakened by the sealing magic, he could still manage shadow manipulation. Darkness poured from his scales like spilled ink, mixing with the morning mist to create an impenetrable veil that swallowed the entire clearing.

Now they were all blind.

But Kaela had spent the last week learning to work with Ashfang through their bond, learning to sense his position and intentions without relying on sight. She knew exactly where he was, could feel his pain and determination through their connection.

More importantly, she could feel where he wasn't.

Fire bloomed in her hands again, but this time it wasn't random sparks. This was precise, controlled, surgical. She sent flicker bursts through the smoke—not to blind, but to illuminate. Each brief flash revealed the positions of their enemies for just long enough to track their movements.

The senior Hunter was moving toward where he thought Ashfang had fallen. Calior was preparing another stone barrier to cut off escape routes. Pyrris was circling overhead, trying to get above the smoke cloud.

And none of them were watching the exile girl they'd dismissed as a secondary threat.

Kaela moved through the darkness like she'd been born to it, guided by the bond and her growing understanding of how shadows and flame could work together. She reached the Hunter just as he raised his spear for what he clearly intended to be a finishing blow.

"Excuse me," she said politely, and set his weapon on fire.

Not the whole spear—that would have been wasteful. Just the rune-carved crystal tip, which turned out to be remarkably flammable when exposed to concentrated heat. The containment magic died with a sound like breaking glass, and suddenly Ashfang was back to full strength.

The senior Hunter stared at his ruined weapon for exactly one second before diving sideways, probably expecting Ashfang to come roaring out of the smoke for revenge.

Instead, Ashfang appeared beside Kaela, shadows still wreathing his form but his ember eyes bright with approval.

"Nice work," he said. "Now, about that escape route..."

The stone barriers Calior had raised were impressive, but they'd been designed to pen in ground-bound prey. They did nothing to address the narrow ravine that cut through the forest about thirty yards to their east—a gap too wide for humans to jump, but perfectly manageable for a demon who could use shadows to extend his leap.

"Can you make it?" Kaela asked, eyeing the distance.

"With you? Absolutely. Trust me?"

It was, Kaela realized, not even a question anymore. "Always."

Ashfang's shadows wrapped around her like a living cloak, and then they were moving—not running, but flowing across the forest floor like smoke given purpose. Behind them, she heard the Hunters shouting orders, heard Calior's hooves ringing against stone as the great stag tried to follow.

But they were already at the ravine's edge, and Ashfang's leap carried them across with room to spare. They landed on the far side in a crouch, Kaela's heart hammering but her smile fierce with triumph.

"They'll track us," she said as they put distance between themselves and their pursuers.

"Let them try." Ashfang's mental voice carried grim satisfaction. "They came hunting an exile and her uncontrolled demon. What they found was a team."

As they moved deeper into the Wilds, Kaela found herself thinking about that word. Team. Not exile and demon, not human and spirit, but partners who could fight together and watch each other's backs.

"We're not running anymore," she said suddenly.

Ashfang's step never faltered, but she felt his attention through the bond. "Oh?"

"I mean, we're running right now because tactical retreat is smart. But we're done being hunted." Kaela's hands still tingled with residual fire, and her confidence had never felt more solid. "Next time they come for us, we're ready."

"Next time," Ashfang agreed, "they'd better bring more than three Hunters and a sealing spear."

As they disappeared into the morning mist, Kaela couldn't help but grin. For the first time since her exile, she felt like she was exactly where she belonged.

Chapter 6: Shadebond Camp

The arrows appeared first—six of them, sprouting from the ground in a perfect circle around Kaela and Ashfang like the world's most pointed suggestion to stop walking.

"Well," Ashfang said conversationally, not even breaking stride, "that was almost polite. Usually people start with the shouting."

Kaela froze, hands automatically moving toward the flames that waited beneath her skin. Around them, the forest had gone suspiciously quiet—no bird calls, no rustling leaves, just the kind of silence that meant they were being watched by people who knew how to stay hidden.

"Identify yourselves." The voice came from somewhere above and to the left, carefully neutral. "What business do exiles have in our territory?"

"The usual exile business," Kaela called back, surprised by how steady her voice sounded. "Trying not to die, mostly. We're just passing through."

A figure dropped from the canopy with liquid grace—a girl maybe a year older than Kaela, dressed in mottled leather that seemed to shift color with the forest shadows. Her dark hair was braided with what looked like bone charms, and her eyes held the kind of wariness that came from surviving things that would have broken softer people.

More importantly, coiled around her shoulders like a living necklace was a serpent the color of swamp water, its scales gleaming with an oily iridescence that suggested things best left unnamed.

"Demon-bonded," the girl observed, taking in Ashfang's horned silhouette. "Recent exile, by the look of your gear. Still carrying Calyss trail rations and city-soft boots." Her gaze sharpened. "You're the one who bonded at Naming Day. The one who made the Council scramble their Hunters."

"News travels fast out here," Kaela said carefully.

"Bad news always does. I'm Dax." She gestured to the serpent, which raised its head to study them with unsettling intelligence. "This is Mireclaw. And you're standing in the middle of territory claimed by people who have very good reasons not to trust strangers."

More figures emerged from concealment—a dozen demon-bonded exiles, their spirits ranging from a shadow-wreathed bat to something that looked like a wolf crossed with a nightmare. They moved with the coordinated precision of a pack, surrounding Kaela and Ashfang without appearing overtly threatening.

Yet.

"We don't want trouble," Kaela said, very aware of how outnumbered they were. "We're just trying to find somewhere safe to—"

"Safe?" Dax's laugh was sharp as broken glass. "There is no safe for people like us. There's only careful, quick, and lucky." She tilted her head, studying Kaela with predatory focus. "Question is, which one are you?"

Ashfang shifted beside her, shadows beginning to gather around his claws. Through their bond, Kaela felt his readiness for violence, his assessment of threats and escape routes. But she also felt something else—curiosity. These weren't random bandits or wild spirits. These were people like them, demon-bonded exiles who'd found a way to survive together.

"I'd like to think I'm all three," Kaela said. "But I'm probably still learning."

"Learning." Dax's expression shifted, something that might have been approval flickering across her features. "At least you're honest about it. Most fresh exiles stumble in here convinced they're destined for greatness, ready to lead us all to glorious victory against the Council."

"And then?"

"And then they get themselves killed doing something stupid and heroic, usually within a week." Dax's hand rested casually on the hilt of a curved blade that gleamed with the same oily sheen as her serpent's scales. "We've learned to be... selective about who we let stay."

The threat was clear, but so was the opportunity. These people had created something in the Wilds— not just survival, but community. A place where demon-bonded exiles could exist without constantly looking over their shoulders.

"What kind of test?" Kaela asked.

Dax's grin revealed teeth that had been filed to points. "The kind that draws first blood."

The clearing they led her to was obviously purpose-built for this—a roughly circular space surrounded by logs for seating, the ground worn smooth by countless feet. The other exiles settled around the perimeter with the casual air of people watching a familiar entertainment.

"Rules are simple," Dax explained as she and Mireclaw took position on one side of the circle. "First blood wins. No killing shots, no permanent maiming. Demons can participate, but they follow the same rules." Her eyes glinted with anticipation. "Any questions?"

"Just one," Kaela said, flexing her fingers and feeling fire respond. "When you say first blood, do you mean first drop, or first actual injury?"

"First drop. We're not savages." Dax's blade sang as it cleared its sheath. "Though if you're hoping for a gentle introduction to our little family, you're going to be disappointed."

The fight began without ceremony. Dax moved like water given violent purpose, her blade tracing patterns in the air that left trails of sickly green mist. Mireclaw uncoiled from her shoulders and flowed across the ground, faster than anything that size had a right to be.

Kaela backpedaled, sending controlled bursts of flame toward the serpent while keeping one eye on Dax's approach. The fires hissed and steamed when they met Mireclaw's toxic aura, creating clouds of vapor that made her eyes water.

"Nice try," Dax called, circling to the left while her demon flanked right. "But poison doesn't burn as easily as you'd think."

She lunged, blade aimed for Kaela's shoulder—a precise strike designed to end things quickly. But Kaela had been training with Ashfang for a week, learning to read movements and anticipate attacks. She twisted aside, letting the blade pass inches from her ribs, and responded with a gout of flame that should have singed Dax's eyebrows.

Should have, but didn't. Because Mireclaw was there, rearing up between them with fangs dripping venom that hissed when it hit the ground.

"Ashfang!" Kaela called, not taking her eyes off the serpent.

"With pleasure."

Shadows erupted from the ground beneath Mireclaw, wrapping around the demon like grasping fingers. The serpent twisted and struck, but Ashfang was already moving, flowing around the clearing's edge with predatory grace.

The match devolved into a complex dance—Dax and Mireclaw working together with the seamless coordination of long practice, while Kaela and Ashfang improvised counters based on their newer but rapidly developing partnership.

Fire met poison in spectacular displays of steam and sparks. Shadows tangled with scales in a writhing mass of darkness and green light. Blade work met flame manipulation in a series of exchanges that had the watching exiles calling out appreciative commentary.

But it was Dax's experience against Kaela's determination, and experience was winning. The older girl's blade work was flawless, her timing perfect, her coordination with Mireclaw so smooth it looked choreographed. Every attack Kaela launched was countered, every opening she thought she saw was actually a trap.

She was losing, and they both knew it.

That's when Mireclaw overcommitted.

The serpent, following up on one of Dax's attacks, lunged for Kaela's ankle with fangs extended. It was a perfect strike, timed to catch her off-balance and end the fight with a single drop of poison-tainted blood.

Kaela could have dodged. Should have dodged. Instead, she planted her feet and caught the serpent's strike with her bare hands.

The venom hit her palms like liquid fire, and she felt the skin begin to blister immediately. But she held on, using her grip to swing Mireclaw around like a living whip, sending the demon crashing into Dax's legs.

Dax stumbled, blade wavering for the first time in the fight. And in that moment of imbalance, Kaela could have ended it. A burst of flame to the face, a tackle while she was off-balance, any number of attacks that would have drawn first blood and won the match.

Instead, she let go of Mireclaw and stepped back, hands smoking but expression calm.

"Yield," she said simply.

The clearing went dead silent. Dax stared at her, confusion and suspicion warring across her features.

"You had me," Dax said finally. "I was open. You could have won."

"Maybe. But your demon was hurt, and mine wasn't. That didn't seem fair." Kaela flexed her blistered hands, wincing slightly. "Besides, I'm not here to prove I can beat you. I'm here to prove I can be trusted."

Dax studied her for a long moment, then looked at her hands, then at Mireclaw, who was coiled defensively around her ankles but otherwise unharmed.

"You're either very smart or very stupid," Dax said finally.

"Probably both."

"Probably." But Dax was smiling now, and it transformed her entire face. "Welcome to the camp, Kaela Veyne. Try not to do anything that gets us all killed."

The watching exiles erupted in cheers and laughter, and suddenly Kaela found herself surrounded by people introducing themselves and their demons, offering commentary on the fight, and generally treating her like she belonged.

It was overwhelming in the best possible way.

"That was well done," said a soft voice beside her. Kaela turned to find a woman in her twenties with gentle eyes and prematurely gray hair. Perched on her shoulder was an owl with feathers that seemed to shift between blue and silver. "I'm Ember Sera, camp healer. This is Thyriel."

"Pleasure to meet you." Kaela held up her blistered hands. "I don't suppose you have anything for—"

"Mireclaw venom? Oh yes, we see that regularly." Ember's smile was warm. "Dax has a tendency to get enthusiastic during sparring matches. Hold still."

The healing was unlike anything Kaela had experienced. Instead of the harsh light she associated with Guardian magic, this was gentle rain that seemed to soak into her skin and carry the pain away. Within moments, the blisters had faded to pink marks that barely stung.

"Rain magic?" Kaela asked, fascinated.

"Thyriel is a storm spirit—the gentle half of thunder and lightning. She specializes in the healing aspects of water." Ember's expression grew thoughtful. "It's interesting, actually. Most people assume demons are purely destructive, but many of them have nurturing aspects that the Council's teachings ignore."

"The Council ignores a lot of things," Dax said, sliding up beside them with Mireclaw draped across her shoulders like a living scarf. She told Kaela about her sentencing, asking who had presided.

"Elder Thorne," Kaela answered.

Dax snorted. "Thorne's a true believer. All fire and purity. He thinks we're a disease to be cleansed. He's the Council's fist, always ready to strike. The one you really have to watch for, though, is Councilor Mirren. He's the mind behind the fist. A politician, subtle and twice as dangerous."

"Speaking of which," Ember said, turning to address the gathered crowd, "I think our new arrivals have earned a proper welcome. What say we break out the good rations and hear their story?"

The cheer that went up was genuinely enthusiastic, and Kaela felt something ease in her chest that she hadn't even realized was tight. For the first time since her exile, she was surrounded by people who understood what she was going through, who didn't see her demon bond as a corruption to be cured.

As the sun set and the camp settled into evening routines, Kaela found herself sitting around a properly built fire pit, sharing stories and laughter with people who felt more like family than most of her blood relatives ever had.

"So what's the plan?" she asked Dax as the crowd began to thin out. "I mean, long term. Do you stay hidden out here forever, or...?"

"Or what? March on Calyss and demand our rights back?" Dax's expression grew serious. "Some of us think about it. But the Council has numbers, resources, training. We have..." She gestured around the camp. "This. It's not nothing, but it's not an army either."

"Maybe it doesn't have to be an army," Kaela said thoughtfully. "Maybe it just has to be proof."

"Proof of what?"

"That demon-bonded people aren't monsters. That we can build something good instead of just surviving." Kaela looked around the camp, taking in the carefully organized living spaces, the communal areas, the sense of purpose that held everything together. "You've already started building it."

Dax followed her gaze, and for a moment, her expression softened. "Maybe. Though building and keeping are different challenges."

As the evening wound down, Ember showed Kaela to a small tent at the edge of the camp. It wasn't much—canvas walls, a bedroll, a small oil lamp—but it was dry and warm and, most importantly, it felt safe.

"Thank you," Kaela said as Ember prepared to leave. "For the healing, for vouching for us, for... all of this."

"Thank me by not doing anything stupid," Ember replied with a smile. "Dax likes you, which means you'll probably fit in well. But this place survives because we're careful. Remember that."

As Kaela settled into her bedroll with Ashfang curled protectively nearby, she felt something she hadn't experienced since before her Naming Day: the absence of fear. Not the temporary reprieve that came from winning a fight or solving an immediate problem, but the deeper peace of knowing she was somewhere she belonged.

"Not bad for a day's work," Ashfang murmured through their bond.

"Not bad at all," Kaela agreed, and for the first time in weeks, she fell asleep without wondering if she'd live to see morning.

Chapter 7: Mirror Lessons

"The first thing you need to understand about demons," Ember said, settling cross-legged in the center of their makeshift classroom, "is that we've been calling them by the wrong name for five hundred years."

Kaela looked around the circle of demon-bonded exiles gathered in the camp's main clearing. There were eight of them this morning—herself, Dax, three others she'd met the night before, and two newcomers who'd arrived just after dawn, looking as shell-shocked as she probably had.

"What should we call them?" asked one of the newcomers, a boy about her age whose nervous energy made the shadow-bat perched on his shoulder flutter restlessly.

"Partners. Reflections. The other half of ourselves." Ember's rain owl, Thyriel, ruffled her blue-silver feathers in what might have been agreement. "But 'demon' is what the Council taught us, so 'demon' is what we're stuck with. The important thing is understanding what they actually are."

Dax lounged against a fallen log, Mireclaw draped across her lap like a living scarf. "Are we doing the mirror talk again? Because honestly, some of us have heard this before."

"Some of you have heard it. Not all of you have understood it." Ember's voice carried the patient authority of someone who'd given this lesson many times. "And our new arrivals need to know this if they're going to survive more than a few weeks."

Ashfang materialized from the shadows behind Kaela, settling beside her with his usual casual disregard for dramatic entrances. Through their bond, she felt his interest—this wasn't just camp orientation, this was something he wanted her to understand.

"Mirrors," Ember continued, "show us things we might not want to see. They reflect what we are, not what we think we are or what we wish we were." She gestured to Thyriel, who hooted softly. "My owl reflects my need to heal, to nurture, to fix what's broken. But she also reflects my tendency to ignore my own needs while caring for others."

"And Mireclaw?" Kaela asked, genuinely curious.

Dax's expression grew thoughtful. "Shows me that I'm more dangerous than I like to admit. That I've got poison in me—anger, mostly—that I use to keep people at a distance." She scratched under the serpent's chin with surprising gentleness. "But also that I'm protective. Poison can be medicine in the right dose."

"The Council teaches that demons are evil spirits that corrupt their hosts," Ember said. "But that's backwards. Demons don't create darkness—they reflect the darkness that's already there. The parts of ourselves we'd rather pretend don't exist."

One of the veterans, a girl with intricate scars covering her arms and a spider-like creature perched on her shoulder, snorted. "So we're bonded to our psychological problems? That's comforting."

"Not our problems," Ember corrected gently. "Our wholeness. Light and shadow both. The Council wants us to believe that purity is possible, that we can cut away the parts of ourselves we don't like and somehow become complete. But that's like trying to have a day with no night, or a coin with only one side."

She stood, moving to the center of the circle. "Today, we're going to practice seeing ourselves clearly. It's not comfortable work, but it's necessary if you want to understand your bond instead of just surviving it."

Kaela felt a chill that had nothing to do with the morning air. "What kind of practice?"

"Fear-trials. Controlled encounters with demons who specialize in showing us what we'd rather not see." Ember's expression grew serious. "Completely voluntary, and we stop the moment anyone asks. But if you're willing to look, you might learn something important about yourself."

The first volunteer was the boy with the shadow-bat. His trial involved facing a demon that looked like a living void with too many eyes—something that whispered every self-doubt and inadequacy he'd ever felt. It lasted maybe thirty seconds before he called for it to stop, but when it was over, his bat was perched more confidently on his shoulder, and his hands had stopped shaking.

"Better?" Ember asked.

"Different," he said, echoing what Kaela had felt after her first real training session with Ashfang. "Like... like I can see the shape of it now, instead of just feeling overwhelmed."

Dax went next, facing a demon that took the form of everyone she'd ever failed to protect. It was brutal to watch—the serpent girl who'd seemed so confident and dangerous reduced to tears within minutes. But when it ended, she and Mireclaw moved together with even smoother coordination than before.

"Kaela?" Ember asked gently. "You don't have to, but..."

"I'll do it." The words came out steadier than she felt. Through the bond, she felt Ashfang's concern, his readiness to intervene if things went wrong. "What do I need to know?"

"This one is called Hollow-Eyes. It feeds on abandonment fears, rejection wounds, the terror of being truly alone." Ember's voice grew softer. "It won't hurt you physically, but emotionally... just remember that whatever you see, whatever you feel, we're all here with you."

The demon that emerged from the forest's edge was perhaps the most unsettling thing Kaela had ever seen. It looked almost human—too almost human, like someone had tried to draw a person from memory and gotten all the proportions slightly wrong. Its eyes were empty sockets that seemed to drink light, and when it moved, it left no shadow.

"Hello, Kaela," it said in a voice like wind through empty houses. "I've been waiting for you."

The scream hit her before she could prepare for it.

Not a sound—that would have been manageable. This was pure fear given voice, the concentrated essence of every time she'd ever felt unwanted, unloved, left behind. It bypassed her ears entirely and struck directly at the part of her brain that remembered being five years old and convinced her parents had forgotten to pick her up from lessons.

Every rejection crashed over her in a wave: classmates who'd found excuses not to include her, teachers who'd looked through her like she wasn't there, the careful politeness of people who couldn't quite bring themselves to be cruel but had no interest in being kind.

You called for any spirit that would have you, Hollow-Eyes whispered, circling her like a predator. *Any spirit at all. Do you know how desperate that sounds? How pathetic?*

The words hit like physical blows because they were true. She had been desperate. She had been willing to bond with anything rather than face the possibility of being Hollow, of being nobody special at all.

Even your demon doesn't really want you, the creature continued, its empty gaze fixed on Ashfang. *He answered because he was lonely, not because you're worthy. The moment something better comes along, he'll abandon you just like everyone else.*

Fire erupted from Kaela's hands—not controlled, not directed, just wild rage that turned the air around her into a furnace. She could hear Ember calling her name, feel Ashfang trying to reach her through their bond, but the fury was too loud, too all-consuming.

There it is, Hollow-Eyes crooned. *The rage you pretend isn't there. The fury at being overlooked, underestimated, forgotten. You want to burn them all, don't you? Everyone who ever made you feel small.*

"Stop," Kaela gasped, but the flames only grew hotter.

You can't stop. This is who you really are—a girl so afraid of being nothing that she'd rather be a monster.

The fire was getting out of control, reaching toward the trees, toward her friends. She was going to hurt someone, going to prove that Hollow-Eyes was right, that she was dangerous and destructive and—

"Kaela." Ashfang's voice cut through the chaos, calm and steady. "Look at me."

She turned, expecting to see disappointment or fear or confirmation of everything Hollow-Eyes had been saying. Instead, she saw understanding.

"Yes," he said simply. "You're angry. Yes, you're afraid of being abandoned. Yes, you want to matter so badly it hurts." His ember eyes never left hers. "And yes, you're learning to channel that into something useful instead of just burning everything down."

The flames began to settle, drawn back by his certainty.

"I am afraid," Kaela said, the words torn from somewhere deep in her chest. "I'm terrified that I'm nobody special, that I'll live my whole life without mattering to anyone. And when I get scared, I get angry, and when I get angry, I want to burn things until people pay attention."

"There we go," Ashfang said, and his silhouette seemed to soften somehow, becoming less sharp-edged and threatening. "Feel it, name it, channel it."

The fire in her hands transformed—still fierce, but controlled now, purposeful. She could feel the abandonment rage that had been driving her, could see the shape of her fear clearly for the first time. But she could also feel something else: the bond that connected her to Ashfang, solid and unbreakable.

He hadn't answered her call because he was desperate. He'd answered because he recognized something in her desperation that matched his own. They were both tired of being alone, both ready to fight for a place to belong.

"Feel," she said, testing the words. "Name. Channel." She looked around the circle at the other demon-bonded exiles, all of them watching with understanding rather than judgment. "Balance."

"Feel, name, channel, balance," Ember repeated, nodding approvingly. "That's our credo here. Not because it's easy, but because it works."

Hollow-Eyes had faded back into the forest shadows, its work done. The fear-trial was over, but its effects lingered. Kaela felt raw, exposed, like she'd been turned inside out and examined. But she also felt clearer somehow, more solid.

"How do you feel?" Dax asked as the group began to disperse.

"Like I've been through a storm," Kaela said honestly. "But like I survived it."

"That's the point. Can't learn to dance with your demons if you're too afraid to look at them." Dax's expression grew thoughtful. "Though I have to say, that abandonment rage of yours burns remarkably clean when you're not trying to pretend it doesn't exist."

As they walked back toward the main camp, Ashfang fell into step beside her. "Better?" he asked.

"Different," she said, using their familiar refrain. "I can see the shape of it now. The fear, the anger, the way they feed each other." She glanced at him sideways. "Did you know? When you answered my call, did you know what you were getting into?"

"I knew you were desperate and angry and tired of being invisible," he said matter-of-factly. "I knew you'd rather risk everything than accept being nothing." His ember eyes met hers. "Those seemed like good qualities in a partner."

"Even if they make me dangerous?"

"Especially if they make you dangerous. Dangerous people get things done." Ashfang's grin showed those obsidian-dagger teeth. "The trick is being dangerous to the right things."

As they rejoined the life of the camp, the fragile peace was broken by a sharp whistle from one of the sentries. A tense energy rippled through the exiles as a heavily laden cart, pulled by a sweat-soaked ox, rumbled into the main clearing. The man driving it was thin and wiry, with eyes that darted nervously toward the shadows.

"Kade," Dax said, her voice a mixture of relief and tension. "You're late."

The man, Kade Thistle, jumped down from the cart, wiping grime from his brow with the back of a leather glove. "The patrols are getting bolder," he rasped, his voice rough with fatigue. "Had to take a three-hour detour through the goblin fens. Nearly lost a wheel."

He began unlashing crates with hurried, efficient movements. "Got the silver-root for Ember and the crystal dust you wanted. Cost me double. My contact says the Council is squeezing all the independent traders."

Kaela watched as the exiles quickly and quietly unloaded the supplies—their lifeline to the outside world. This was Kade, the spirit-trader she'd heard whispers about.

"This is our new arrival, Kaela," Dax said, gesturing to her.

Kade gave her a brief, assessing glance, his eyes lingering on Ashfang. "The one from the Naming Day," he grunted. "You're causing a lot of trouble." It wasn't an accusation, just a statement of fact.

"How's your nephew?" Dax asked, her tone softening slightly.

A flicker of pain crossed Kade's face. "He's keeping his head down in the city. I worry, though. He's a good kid, but... impressionable." He shook his head, pushing the thought away. "I can't stay. The longer I'm here, the bigger the risk."

Within minutes, the cart was empty and Kade was preparing to leave. After he disappeared back into the woods, Dax turned to Kaela.

"Kade's network is how we survive," she explained quietly. "But he's right to be paranoid. If the Council ever connects him to us..." She left the sentence unfinished, the implication hanging heavy in the air.

Chapter 8: Discipline over Flare

Dawn in the Shadebond camp came with the sound of controlled explosions.

Kaela stood in the training circle they'd cleared at the camp's edge, sweat beading on her forehead despite the cool morning air. Around her, scorch marks in the dirt told the story of six weeks of intensive practice—some precise and purposeful, others considerably less so.

"Again," Ashfang said from his position across the circle. "Breath first, then flame. Feel the rhythm."

Kaela closed her eyes and found her center—four counts in, hold for two, six counts out. It was a pattern they'd developed together, syncing her breathing with the natural ebb and flow of Ashfang's ember-heart. Through their bond, she could feel his steady pulse, like a metronome made of fire and shadow.

When she opened her eyes, flame danced in her palms—not the wild, chaotic inferno of her early attempts, but something controlled and purposeful. She held it steady for a count of ten, then let it fade without dramatics.

"Better," Ashfang acknowledged. "Now show me precision."

This was the part she'd been struggling with. Kaela extended her hands and began the exercise they'd dubbed 'flame-writing'—creating controlled bursts of fire that traced specific patterns in the air. Letters, geometric shapes, even simple pictures if she was feeling ambitious.

Today's assignment was her name in the old script, the formal lettering used for ceremonial documents. Each stroke required perfect timing, exact heat control, and the kind of steady hand that came from hours of practice. A dull ache began to form behind her eyes, the familiar price of sustained concentration. This was a different kind of cost than raw power... not a draining, but a sharpening, a focus so intense it felt like it could wear grooves into her mind.

K-A-E-L-A.

The letters hung in the air for a moment, glowing softly against the morning sky, before fading to wisps of smoke.

"Not bad," said a voice behind her. Kaela turned to find Dax approaching with Mireclaw coiled around her shoulders like a living scarf. "Though your 'E' is still a bit wobbly."

"Everything's a bit wobbly," Kaela admitted. "But it's getting steadier."

"That's the point," Ashfang said, padding over to join them. "Steady improvement over dramatic gestures. Discipline over flare."

It had become their motto over the past weeks—a conscious rejection of the flashy Guardian displays that dominated Calyss's dueling culture. Those fights were all about spectacle, about overwhelming opponents with raw power and perfect technique. But demon-bonded combat was different. It required subtlety, adaptation, the ability to turn weaknesses into strengths.

"Speaking of discipline," Dax said, "Ember wants to see you after breakfast. Something about a field test."

Kaela's stomach dropped. Field tests in the Shadebond camp were notorious for being educational, challenging, and occasionally terrifying. The last one had involved navigating a maze while blindfolded, guided only by her bond with Ashfang. She'd passed, but barely, and had walked into more trees than she cared to remember.

"What kind of field test?"

"The kind where you prove you can actually use what you've been learning when something's trying to kill you," Dax said cheerfully. "You know, practical application."

An hour later, Kaela found herself following Ember deeper into the Wilds than she'd ever ventured before. The healer moved through the twisted forest with the confidence of someone who knew every root and stone, while Thyriel scouted ahead with soft hoots of warning or encouragement.

"Where exactly are we going?" Kaela asked as they picked their way around a particularly treacherous ravine.

"Gnashroot territory," Ember replied calmly. "There's a young one that's been causing problems for the supply runs—nothing dangerous, just aggressive and territorial. Perfect for testing whether you can handle a real threat without reverting to panic-fire."

Ashfang materialized beside them with his usual dramatic flair. "Gnashroot. Hunger demons. They drain spiritual energy through direct contact and have a tendency to charge first and think never."

"Sounds delightful," Kaela muttered. "Any weaknesses?"

"They're not particularly intelligent, and they're vulnerable to precise strikes rather than overwhelming force," Ember explained. "The trick is staying calm enough to find the opening."

They found the Gnashroot in a clearing dominated by a massive oak tree whose roots had been gnawed into intricate patterns. The demon itself was about the size of a large boar, covered in bark-like hide and sporting tusks that gleamed with an unhealthy light. It was currently demolishing what remained of a fallen log, apparently for the simple joy of destruction.

"Remember," Ember said softly, "the goal isn't to kill it. Just drive it off. These creatures can be reasoned with if you approach them correctly."

"And if reasoning fails?" Kaela asked.

"Then you get creative."

The Gnashroot noticed them about the same time Kaela stepped into the clearing. Its head came up, bark-hide bristling, and its eyes fixed on her with unmistakable hunger. Through her bond with Ashfang, she could feel the creature's spiritual signature—raw appetite wrapped around a core of territorial rage.

"Easy," she said, hands spread in what she hoped was a non-threatening gesture. "We're just passing through. No need for anyone to get—"

The Gnashroot charged.

For a split second, Kaela felt the familiar surge of panic, the instinct to respond with overwhelming force. Fire roared to life in her chest, demanding release, wanting to turn this threat into ash and memory.

But then her training kicked in.

Four counts in. Feel the fear, name it: territorial defense, not malice. Two count hold. This wasn't personal—the demon was just protecting its space. Six counts out. Channel the fire, don't let it channel you.

Instead of meeting the charge head-on, Kaela sidestepped at the last possible moment, letting the Gnashroot's momentum carry it past her. As it skidded to a halt and wheeled around for another attack, she gestured with one hand and created a wall of flame between them—not to burn, but to establish distance.

"That's your territory," she said calmly, pointing to the area behind the fire wall. "This is mine. We can share the clearing, or you can keep charging into flames. Your choice."

The Gnashroot stared at her through the wall of fire, breathing heavily. She could see the intelligence in its eyes, the moment when it realized she wasn't trying to dominate or drive it away—just establish boundaries.

After a long moment, it snorted and turned back to its log-gnawing, pointedly ignoring the humans in its clearing.

"Well done," Ember said, and there was genuine pride in her voice. "You read the situation instead of just reacting to it."

Kaela let the fire wall fade, feeling drained but satisfied. "It wasn't trying to hurt us. It was just... scared. Protecting something it cared about."

"Most aggression is fear wearing a mask," Ashfang observed. "The trick is seeing through the mask to what's really happening underneath."

As they made their way back toward camp, Kaela found herself thinking about that moment of choice—the split second when she could have unleashed everything she had, could have turned fear into fury and fury into flame. It would have been easier, in some ways. Certainly more dramatic.

But it wouldn't have been right.

"I cried after my first real fight," she said suddenly. "With the wild hounds, when we were still running from the Hunters. Ashfang asked me why, and I said it was because I felt terrible about killing things."

"And now?" Ember asked.

"Now I think it was because I enjoyed it." The admission came easier than she'd expected. "The moment when everything clicked, when we moved together like we'd been partners for years instead of hours. It felt..." She searched for the right word. "It felt like coming home."

"That's not a bad thing," Ashfang said gently. "Partnership is supposed to feel right. The bond is supposed to complete something that was missing."

"But it scared me. The idea that I could enjoy violence, that I could be good at it." Kaela kicked at a loose stone as they walked. "I thought that made me a monster."

"What do you think now?"

Kaela considered the question as they navigated around the ravine they'd crossed earlier. Below them, water trickled over smooth stones, and somewhere in the distance, she could hear the sound of the camp's daily activities—people living, working, building something together.

"I think there's a difference between enjoying violence and enjoying competence," she said finally. "What I liked wasn't the fighting—it was the feeling that I was finally good at something that mattered. That I could protect people, could contribute something valuable." "There we go," Ashfang rumbled approvingly. "Feel, name, channel, balance."

"The grief wasn't about the violence," Kaela continued, the pieces clicking into place as she spoke. "It was about losing the person I used to be. The girl who thought she was ordinary, who believed that extraordinary meant perfect." She looked at her hands, where small flames danced without her conscious direction. "I was mourning who I thought I was supposed to be." "And who are you actually?" Ember asked.

Kaela smiled, feeling something settle into place inside her chest. "Someone who can stand in a clearing with a territorial demon and find a solution that doesn't require anyone to get hurt. Someone who can shape fire instead of being shaped by it."

"Now we shape the fire," Ashfang agreed, echoing words he'd spoken weeks ago in very different circumstances. "We don't escape it or suppress it or pretend it doesn't exist. We work with it."

As they crested the final hill before camp, Kaela felt the truth of those words settle into her bones. The fire inside her wasn't something to be afraid of or ashamed of—it was part of who she was, no different from her stubbornness or her compassion or her tendency to overthink everything.

The trick wasn't controlling it. The trick was learning to dance with it. And for the first time since her Naming Day, Kaela felt like she was learning the steps.

Chapter 9: Archive Break-In

"This is officially the stupidest plan anyone has ever conceived," Ashfang muttered as they crouched in the ancient aqueduct beneath Calyss. "And I once watched a human try to befriend a wild dragon by offering it a sandwich."

Kaela adjusted her grip on the water-slicked stone, trying not to think about the fifty-foot drop to the drainage channels below. "Do you have a better idea for getting into the city archives without being seen?"

"Several. Most of them involve significantly less crawling through century-old sewage systems."

"These aren't sewers," Dax corrected from ahead of them, her voice echoing strangely in the tunnel. "They're aqueducts. There's a difference."

"The smell suggests otherwise."

It had been Dax's idea to infiltrate the archives, motivated by Kaela's growing questions about the true history of demon bonds. If they were going to challenge the Council's narrative, they needed evidence—real proof that the official story about demons being corrupted spirits was a lie.

The camp had been split on the wisdom of such a mission. Half the exiles thought it was suicide; the other half thought it was pointless. But Ember had quietly provided them with detailed maps of the old aqueduct system, and after three days of planning, here they were: crawling through stone tunnels toward the heart of Calyss like the world's most reluctant urban explorers.

"Light ahead," Dax whispered, holding up a hand for silence.

Through the grating at the tunnel's end, Kaela could see the soft golden glow of Guardian lanterns—the eternal flames that lit Calyss's underground passages. The archives were built into the foundation of the Citadel itself, protected by layers of both mundane and magical security.

Fortunately, whoever had designed those defenses hadn't anticipated an attack from below.

"Guardian patrol," Dax observed, watching shadows move past the light. "Two guards, spirits look like... crystal stag and ember hawk. Standard patrol pattern."

Kaela closed her eyes, reaching out through her bond with Ashfang. His senses were sharper than hers, better adapted to the darkness and stone. Through him, she could feel the rhythmic footsteps of the guards, the warm glow of their Guardian spirits, the ebb and flow of their patrol route.

"They pass this grating every twelve minutes," she whispered. "We'll have maybe eight minutes between passes to get inside and find cover."

"Eight minutes to break into the most secure building in the city," Ashfang said. "What could possibly go wrong?"

The grating came away easier than expected—apparently, centuries of moisture had corroded the mounting bolts past the point of structural integrity. They slipped through the opening one at a time, emerging into a storage corridor lined with racks of ceremonial robes and religious artifacts.

The archives themselves lay beyond a heavy oak door marked with the Council's sunburst seal. Kaela expected locks, magical wards, guardian spirits on permanent watch duty. Instead, she found a simple latch and a sign reading: "Authorized Personnel Only."

"That's it?" she whispered. "That's their idea of security?"

"Why would they need more?" Dax pointed out. "Until about five minutes ago, the only people who could get this far were Council loyalists with legitimate business here."

The archives were vast—a honeycomb of chambers carved directly into the Citadel's foundation, filled with scrolls, books, tablets, and murals that chronicled five centuries of Calyss's official history. Golden lanterns cast everything in warm, reverent light, making the space feel more like a temple than a library.

Which, Kaela realized, was probably the point.

"What exactly are we looking for?" Ashfang asked, his shadows helping to muffle their footsteps as they moved deeper into the collection.

"Anything about the Great Sundering," Kaela said. "The real story, not the sanitized version they teach in schools."

They split up to cover more ground, each taking a different section of the archives. Kaela found herself in a chamber devoted to pre-Sundering history, its walls covered with murals that made her stop dead in her tracks.

The paintings showed spirits unlike anything she'd seen before—massive, majestic beings that seemed to combine light and shadow in impossible harmony. A wolf whose coat shifted from golden sunlight to midnight darkness. A serpent with scales that gleamed like stars against a void. A great owl whose feathers contained both storm clouds and clear skies.

"Eidolons," she breathed, recognizing the creatures from half-remembered legends.

But something was wrong with the murals. Tool marks scarred the painted surface—deliberate chisel strikes that had removed faces, obscured details, carved away sections of the images. Someone had taken great care to damage these paintings without destroying them entirely.

Someone who wanted to hide the truth but preserve enough evidence to find it again.

"Kaela." Dax's voice carried from the next chamber, tight with urgency. "You need to see this."

She found Dax standing before a wall covered in official documents—decrees, proclamations, legislative acts sealed with wax and ribbon. But it was the scroll in Dax's hands that made Kaela's blood run cold.

"By order of the Emergency Council of Light, in response to the Spiritual Crisis of the Third Age, all Eidolon manifestations are hereby declared unstable and dangerous to public safety. Immediate severance protocols are authorized. The Great Sundering shall commence at the summer solstice. May the light preserve us all."

The document was signed by twelve names, each accompanied by an official seal. At the bottom, in smaller text, was a date: five hundred years ago, almost to the day.

"They did it on purpose," Kaela whispered. "The Sundering wasn't some natural disaster or spiritual crisis. It was a deliberate act."

A low growl rumbled from the shadows beside her. "I knew it was a catastrophe," Ashfang's voice echoed in her mind, laced with a fresh, five-hundred-year-old fury. "I felt the world tear itself apart. But I always believed it was a natural disaster, a spiritual plague that the Council took advantage of to seize power. To think they *caused* it... that this was a choice..." The raw hatred in his tone made Kaela flinch. This was no longer just about their freedom; it was about vengeance for an ancient crime.

"Gets better," Dax said grimly, holding up another scroll. "Listen to this: 'Population control measures have exceeded expectations. Severed spirits show

73% compliance rates compared to 12% for integrated Eidolons. Recommend permanent implementation of dual-classification system.'"

Kaela felt sick. "Population control measures?"

"They split the spirits because whole spirits were harder to control. Eidolons were too independent, too powerful, too willing to question authority." Dax's hands were shaking with barely controlled rage. "So they broke them in half, branded one half evil, and convinced everyone it was for their own protection."

"There's more." Ashfang's voice came from deeper in the archives, where he'd been investigating the oldest sections. "You really need to see this."

They found him standing before a mural that had somehow escaped the systematic defacement. It showed the Great Sundering itself—not as a salvation, but as a catastrophe. Eidolons writhed in agony as some kind of magical ritual tore them apart, their light and shadow halves falling to earth like broken stars.

And standing around the ritual circle, wearing the ceremonial robes of the Council of Light, were figures that looked disturbingly familiar.

"Is that...?" Kaela began.

"Councilor Mirren's great-great-grandfather," Dax confirmed, pointing to one of the painted figures. "And that's definitely the Brightwind family crest on that robe. The founding families of the Council—they were the ones who performed the Sundering."

Alarm bells began to ring somewhere in the distance.

"Time to go," Ashfang said, shadows already wreathing around him. "Now would be good."

They moved fast, grabbing what documents they could carry and heading for the storage corridor. But the way back to their aqueduct entrance was blocked—Guardian light flooded the passage, and they could hear armored footsteps approaching from multiple directions.

"This way," Dax hissed, leading them deeper into the Citadel's foundation. "There's got to be another way out."

They found it in the reliquary—a chamber filled with religious artifacts and, more importantly, a ventilation shaft that led to the surface. The climb was harrowing, made worse by the sounds of pursuit echoing through the building above them, but they emerged into an alley behind the Citadel just as the sun was setting.

"That was too close," Dax panted as they put distance between themselves and the Citadel. "They'll have the whole city searching for us within the hour."

"Worth it," Kaela said firmly, clutching the scrolls they'd managed to rescue. "This changes everything. This proves that the Council has been lying for five centuries."

"Proving it and getting people to believe it are different challenges," Ashfang pointed out.

"Especially when those people have been raised from birth to see demons as inherently evil."

Kaela looked back at the Citadel, its towers rising into the darkening sky like accusations against the stars. She thought about the murals, the deliberate defacement, the careful preservation of evidence that indicted the Council's foundational myths.

"We're not going to burn it down," she said quietly. "The Citadel, the Council, the whole system. We're going to do something worse."

"Which is?" Dax asked.

"We're going to tell the truth. We're going to show people what really happened, what was really taken from them." Kaela's hands flickered with controlled flame as she spoke. "And we're going to give them the choice to reclaim it."

As they melted back into the shadows of the Wilds, carrying proof of the greatest lie ever told, Kaela felt something shift inside her. This wasn't about survival anymore, or even acceptance. This was about justice.

And justice, she was learning, burned a lot hotter than revenge.

Chapter 10: The Amnesty Trap

The message arrived with the morning patrol reports, delivered by a Guardian-bonded messenger who looked like he'd rather be anywhere else in the world.

"Kaela Veyne," he announced, his voice carrying across the camp with formal precision. "By order of the Council of Light, you are hereby offered terms of amnesty and safe return to Calyss."

Kaela looked up from the training notes she'd been reviewing, a chill running down her spine that had nothing to do with the morning air. Around her, the camp had gone dead silent—conversations cut off mid-sentence, work stopped mid-task. Even the demons seemed to sense the tension, pressing closer to their bonded partners.

"What terms?" she asked, though she was pretty sure she already knew.

The messenger unrolled an official scroll, complete with the Council's seal and enough ribbons to outfit a parade. "The Council recognizes that your... incident... at the Naming Day ceremony may have been the result of youthful desperation rather than deliberate corruption. In the spirit of mercy, they offer you the opportunity to return home, receive proper healing, and rejoin civilized society."

"Why?" Kaela cut in, her voice sharp. "Why just me?"

The messenger's expression became more calculated. "Your public bonding has made you a symbol," he admitted. "Your defiance has given hope to other corrupted individuals. By publicly accepting the Council's mercy and undergoing purification, you will become a different kind of symbol—one that demonstrates that our methods work, that redemption is possible through order. It would be a powerful tool for discouraging future rebellions."

"And the catch?" Dax asked from beside her, Mireclaw's scales shifting to a more aggressive pattern.

"The demon bond must be severed," the messenger continued, as if discussing the weather. "The creature will be properly contained, and you will undergo a purification ritual to ensure no lingering contamination."

The casual way he said 'creature' made Kaela's hands clench into fists. Through their bond, she felt Ashfang's sardonic amusement—he'd expected this, probably from the moment they'd bonded.

"How generous," Ashfang drawled, materializing from the shadows with his usual dramatic flair. "Tell me, messenger boy, what happens to demons who get 'properly contained'?"

The messenger's face went pale, but he held his ground. "That's not your concern. The offer is for Kaela Veyne only."

"Everything concerning her concerns me," Ashfang replied, his voice dropping to something dangerously soft. "We're bonded. Permanently. That's how this works."

"Bonds can be severed," the messenger insisted. "The Council has developed new techniques—"

"The Council has developed new ways to torture spirits," Ember interrupted, stepping into the circle with Thyriel perched on her shoulder. "We've seen the refugees from their 'purification' attempts. Half-dead humans with phantom pain that never stops, spirits driven insane by forced separation."

Kaela stood up slowly, feeling the weight of every eye in the camp. This wasn't just about her anymore—it was about what the Shadebond community represented, about whether demon-bonded people had the right to exist as they were or would always be seen as problems to be solved.

"I need to see the full terms," she said.

The messenger handed over the scroll with obvious relief, probably eager to get this conversation over with. Kaela read through the formal language, translating the bureaucratic euphemisms into plain truth:

Return to Calyss meant house arrest under Council supervision. 'Healing' meant magical torture designed to rip away half her soul. 'Rejoining civilized society' meant accepting that who she was now was fundamentally wrong and needed to be fixed.

And Ashfang...

"What does 'properly contained' actually mean?" she asked.

The messenger shifted uncomfortably. "The creature would be returned to secure holding, where it can't harm anyone else."

"That's not an answer."

"The details aren't—"

"The details are everything," Kaela cut him off. "You're asking me to trade my partner's freedom for the chance to pretend the last two months never happened. I want to know exactly what you're offering and exactly what you're asking for."

The messenger looked around the camp, clearly hoping someone else would handle this conversation. When no help appeared, he sighed and pulled out a second scroll.

"Fine. The demon would be placed in crystalline suspension—a form of magical stasis that prevents it from influencing others while preserving its existence. It's completely humane."

"Humane," Dax repeated flatly. "Like keeping a person in a coma for the rest of eternity."

"It's not a person—"

"Yes, he is." The words came out of Kaela with absolute certainty. "Ashfang is a person. He thinks, he feels, he makes choices. He's saved my life more times than I can count, and he's never asked for anything in return except the chance to exist freely."

Through their bond, she felt Ashfang's surprise, followed quickly by something that felt like gratitude.

"The Council is offering you a chance to come home," the messenger pressed. "To see your parents again, to have a normal life—"

"Define normal," Kaela said. "Because from where I'm standing, normal means lying about who I am, pretending that half my soul doesn't exist, and letting the people I care about be locked in magical cages for the crime of being inconvenient."

She looked around the camp—at Dax and her poison serpent, at Ember and her storm owl, at all the other demon-bonded exiles who'd found a way to build something good out of their rejection by society.

"This is normal," she continued. "People working together, supporting each other, learning to be whole instead of pretending to be pure. The Council wants me to trade that for the chance to be half a person in a world that will never really accept what I am."

"Your parents miss you," the messenger said, playing what he probably thought was his strongest card. "They've been asking about you every day since your exile."

That one hurt. Kaela felt tears prick at her eyes as she thought about her mother's careful stitching, her father's precise handwriting, the note that promised they would always love her.

"I miss them too," she said quietly. "But I won't betray my partner to ease their pain. And I won't pretend that what the Council did to me—to all of us—was justified just because they're offering to undo part of it."

The messenger stared at her for a long moment, clearly struggling to understand how anyone could refuse such a generous offer. Finally, he shook his head and began rolling up his scrolls.

"You're making a mistake," he said. "The Council's patience isn't infinite. This offer won't remain open forever."

"Good," Kaela replied. "Because I'm not interested in their patience. I'm interested in their accountability."

The messenger mounted his Guardian-bonded hawk and lifted off without another word, leaving the camp in thoughtful silence.

"Well," Ashfang said after he'd disappeared into the morning sky, "that was unexpectedly satisfying."

"You thought I'd take it," Kaela accused.

"For about thirty seconds, yes. It would have been the practical choice—return to safety, comfort, family. All you had to do was abandon the inconvenient demon who'd ruined your perfect life."

"You didn't ruin my life," Kaela said firmly. "You saved it. The life I had before was... small. Safe, maybe, but small. I was so afraid of being ordinary that I never tried to be extraordinary."

"And now?"

Kaela looked around the camp again, at the community they'd built, at the evidence of the Council's lies they'd uncovered, at the training ground where she'd learned to shape fire instead of being shaped by it.

"Now I'm learning that extraordinary doesn't mean perfect. It means being brave enough to be whole, even when the world tells you that half of who you are is wrong."

Dax clapped her on the shoulder with enough force to nearly knock her over. "Damn right. Besides, who wants to go back to a place where the best they can offer you is the chance to forget who you've become?"

"The Council will try again," Ember warned. "This was their opening offer—next time, they'll escalate."

"Let them," Kaela said, and was surprised by the steel in her own voice. "We have work to do."

As the camp slowly returned to its daily routines, Kaela found herself thinking about the choice she'd just made. Part of her did want to go home, wanted to see her parents and sleep in her own bed and pretend that none of this had ever happened.

But that was the old Kaela, the one who'd been so desperate to matter that she'd been willing to settle for being noticed. The new Kaela—the one who could stand toe-to-toe with Council messengers and territorial demons alike—had bigger ambitions.

She was going to change the world. And she was going to do it without abandoning the people who'd helped her become someone worth changing it for.

"No regrets?" Ashfang asked as they walked back toward the training grounds.

"Just one," Kaela said.

"Oh?"

"I regret that it took me so long to realize that being whole was an option."

Ashfang's chuckle rumbled through their bond like distant thunder. "Trust me, little fire-starter. You're just getting started."

Chapter 11: Citadel Infiltration

"I know I said the archive mission was the stupidest plan ever conceived," Ashfang muttered as they crouched in the storm drains beneath the Citadel, "but somehow we've managed to top ourselves."

Kaela adjusted her grip on the rope they'd used to descend from the drainage outlet, trying not to think about the fact that they were now directly underneath the most heavily fortified building in Calyss. "The archives gave us proof of what the Council did. We need proof of what they're still doing."

"And you're certain the prisoners are being held here?" Dax whispered, Mireclaw's scales shifting to match the damp stone walls around them.

"The supply manifests we found were pretty specific," Kaela replied. "Medicinal supplies, restraint equipment, and enough food for about fifty people being delivered to sub-basement level three. That's not storage—that's maintenance of living prisoners."

It had taken two weeks to plan this mission, another week to gather intelligence, and considerable argument to convince the camp elders that the risk was worth it. But the documents they'd recovered from the archives painted a disturbing picture: demon-bonded individuals weren't just being exiled anymore. Many were disappearing entirely, taken for what the Council euphemistically called "remedial treatment."

"Motion sensors end at the second sub-level," Dax reported, consulting the building plans they'd acquired through less-than-legal means. "After that, it's just physical security and Guardian patrols."

"Which makes sense," Ashfang observed. "Can't have magical surveillance where you're conducting magical experiments. Too much interference."

The thought of what those experiments might involve made Kaela's stomach clench, but she pushed the fear aside. Feel, name, channel, balance. Fear could be fuel if she used it right.

They moved through the lower levels like ghosts, their demons providing advantages no Guardian-bonded infiltrator could match. Ashfang's shadows muffled their footsteps and hid them from casual observation. Mireclaw's enhanced senses warned them of approaching patrols long before human ears could detect them. And Kaela's precise flame control let them bypass the magical locks without triggering alarms.

Sub-basement level one was storage—crates of supplies, religious artifacts, and the accumulated bureaucratic detritus of five centuries of theocratic rule. Sub-basement level two housed the Citadel's archives, which they'd already visited. But sub-basement level three...

"Cells," Dax breathed as they emerged from the stairwell into a corridor lined with iron doors. "This whole level is a prison."

The hallway stretched into darkness, punctuated by heavy doors with small viewing windows. But what made Kaela's blood run cold wasn't the architecture—it was the silence. No voices, no movement, just the oppressive quiet of a place where hope had gone to die.

"Start checking cells," she whispered. "We need to know who's down here and what's being done to them."

The first few cells were empty, but the fourth contained something that made Kaela's heart nearly stop. A girl perhaps a year younger than herself sat huddled in the corner, wearing the gray robes of a Council penitent. Her eyes were open but vacant, staring at nothing, and when Kaela whispered through the viewing slot, she didn't respond.

"There's something wrong with her," Kaela said, fighting to keep her voice steady. Ashfang pressed closer to the door, his ember eyes glowing softly in the darkness. "Severed. Recently, by the look of it. They cut her bond and left her to deal with the aftermath alone."

"Can we help her?"

"Not here. Not now. She needs healing, time, people who understand what she's been through." His voice carried a weight of old pain. "Forced severance is... traumatic. She might never fully recover."

They moved from cell to cell, finding more of the same—demon-bonded teens and young adults in various stages of magical torture. Some had been severed from their spirits and left hollow. Others showed signs of failed binding attempts, their souls scarred by repeated efforts to force Guardian bonds. A few seemed relatively intact but were clearly being held for future "treatment."

"This is what they mean by remedial care," Dax said, her voice tight with fury. "They're not trying to help these people—they're trying to break them down and rebuild them."

"Into what?" Kaela asked, though she was afraid she already knew. "Perfect citizens. People so traumatized by what was done to them that they'll never question the Council's authority again." They reached the end of the corridor without finding any guards—apparently, the Council felt confident that their prisoners posed no escape risk. Which made sense, given the condition most of them were in.

"We need to get them out," Kaela said. "All of them?" Ashfang's tone was carefully neutral. "That's fifty people, most of whom can barely walk. We'd need transport, medical supplies, safe houses—"

"Then we get those things." Kaela turned to face her partners, her hands flickering with controlled flame. "We can't leave them here. We can't let the Council keep doing this." "The logistics alone—" Dax began.

"Will be complicated. I know. But look at them." Kaela gestured toward the cells. "Look at what's being done in the name of purity and order. Every day we delay is another day these people suffer for the crime of being inconvenient."

She walked back to the cell containing the severed girl, studying the lock mechanism. "Standard iron bars, mechanical tumbler locks, no magical reinforcement at this level. They're relying on the prisoners being too broken to attempt escape."

"Even if we could get them out," Dax said, "where would we take them? The camp can't support fifty refugees, especially not ones who need serious medical care."

"Then we find somewhere that can. Or we make somewhere that can." Kaela's voice grew stronger as she spoke, fueled by righteous anger and protective determination. "The Borderlands have towns that are quietly sympathetic to our cause. Ember knows healers who work outside the Council's oversight. We have resources—we just need to organize them."

Ashfang studied her face in the dim light. "You're talking about a full-scale rescue operation. The kind that gets people killed if it goes wrong." "People are already being killed," Kaela replied. "Just slowly, and quietly, where no one has to see it." She looked down the corridor at the rows of cells. "At least this way, they'll have a chance."

A soft sound echoed from the stairwell—footsteps, moving with the measured pace of a security patrol.

"Time to go," Dax hissed.

They retreated through the corridors like shadows fleeing the dawn, retracing their path through the Citadel's foundations. But as they climbed back up through the storm drains toward the surface, Kaela's mind was already racing ahead to planning and logistics and the hundred details that would need to fall into place for a rescue of this magnitude.

"You're serious about this," Ashfang said as they emerged into the pre-dawn darkness outside the city walls.

"Dead serious." Kaela looked back at the Citadel, its towers silhouetted against the lightening sky. "Those people trusted the Council to help them, and instead they were betrayed, tortured, broken down piece by piece. Someone needs to speak for them."

"Someone," Dax observed, "or you specifically?"

Kaela considered the question as they made their way back toward the Wilds. Why did this feel like her responsibility? She wasn't the oldest or most experienced of the demon-bonded exiles. She wasn't a natural leader or a tactical genius. She was just a girl who'd made a desperate choice at her Naming Day and somehow survived the consequences.

But maybe that was enough. Maybe being willing to try was more important than being perfectly qualified.

"Me specifically," she said finally. "Because I can do something about it, which means I have to do something about it."

"Even if it's dangerous? Even if it might fail?"

"Especially then." Kaela felt the truth of the words settle into her bones. "The Council is counting on us being too afraid, too divided, too broken to fight back. But we're not broken—we're just different. And different doesn't mean wrong."

As they slipped back into the forest, Kaela was already composing the arguments she'd need to make to convince the camp elders. The rescue would require resources they didn't have, coordination they'd never attempted, and risks that could destroy everything they'd built.

But in her mind, she could see the severed girl's vacant eyes, could imagine the other prisoners waiting in their cells for salvation that might never come. The Council had made them into symbols of their own failures, proof that deviation from the approved path led only to suffering.

It was time to show them what deviation could actually accomplish.

"Fifty people," she murmured as they approached the camp's perimeter.

"Fifty people," Ashfang agreed. "This should be interesting."

As they prepared to retreat, Dax held up a hand, her eyes fixed on a small, alcove-like office they had previously ignored. "Wait. Guard station."

Moving with practiced silence, she slipped inside. A moment later, she emerged holding a thin, leather-bound logbook. "Guard rotation schedules," she whispered, flipping through the pages. "And... requisitions."

She stopped on a page, her finger tracing a line of neat script. Kaela and Ashfang leaned in to look.

The entry read: *Requisition #734: One (1) set of Containment Cuffs and one (1) Spirit-Dampening Collar from the Vault of Chains for Subject 34. Subject has shown signs of bond regeneration. Expedited delivery requested.*

"The Vault of Chains," Ashfang breathed, his voice laced with a venom Kaela had never heard before. "I'd heard whispers of such a place. An arsenal of torture devices from the Sundering, designed not just to contain, but to break spirits."

Kaela's blood ran cold. It wasn't enough for the Council to imprison these people; they had a dedicated armory to systematically crush their spirits. "If we're going to get these prisoners out," she said, her voice low and determined, "we can't leave the Council with the tools to do this to others. We have to find that vault."

"That's a different level of security, Kaela," Dax warned. "The prison level is one thing, but an arsenal from the Sundering? It'll be warded against everything we've got."

"Then we'll find a way," Kaela insisted. "Freeing the prisoners is only half the battle if we leave the gun in their captors' hands."

The mission had just become infinitely more complicated. It was no longer just a rescue. It was now a disarmament.

Chapter 12: The Vault of Chains

The Vault of Chains lay three levels deeper than the prison cells, hidden behind wards that made Kaela's skin crawl just approaching them. She pressed herself against the cold stone wall, watching Dax work on the lock with tools that definitely hadn't come from any legitimate source.

"This is taking too long," Ashfang muttered, his shadows writhing with barely contained agitation. "We've been down here for twenty minutes. Someone's going to notice eventually."

"Then maybe you could help instead of just complaining," Dax shot back, sweat beading on her forehead as she manipulated the lock's mechanism. "These aren't normal tumblers—they're warded against demon influence."

It had taken them three weeks to plan this infiltration, building on intelligence gathered from their previous mission. The prisoners they'd found were just the beginning—deeper in the Citadel's foundations lay the Council's real secret weapons. According to the documents they'd stolen, this vault contained the arsenal used to subjugate demon-bonded spirits for five centuries.

"Got it," Dax breathed as the lock finally yielded. The heavy door swung open to reveal a chamber that made Kaela's blood run cold.

The vault was filled with weapons designed specifically to torture spirits. Crystal-tipped spears that could sever bonds from a distance. Chains forged with containment runes that would drain a demon's power until nothing remained but empty shell. Collars designed to force compliance through magical agony. And in the center of it all, mounted on a pedestal like a shrine to cruelty, was something that made even Ashfang recoil in horror.

"Is that...?" Kaela whispered.

"A Master Seal," Ashfang confirmed, his voice hollow with old pain. "I haven't seen one since the Great Sundering. They were used to split the Eidolons—to tear whole spirits into light and shadow halves."

The artifact was beautiful in the way that poisonous flowers were beautiful—a crystal sphere the size of a human head, filled with swirling silver light that seemed to move with predatory intelligence. Runes covered its surface in spiraling patterns that hurt to look at directly.

"The legends said they were all destroyed," Dax said, moving closer despite her obvious reluctance.

"The legends said a lot of things that turned out to be lies," Kaela replied grimly. "The question is, what's it doing here?"

As if in answer to her question, footsteps echoed from the corridor outside. But these weren't the measured steps of a patrol—they were purposeful, confident, belonging to someone who had every right to be in this forbidden place.

"Hide," Ashfang hissed, but it was too late.

Councilor Mirren stepped into the vault, flanked by two Guardian-bonded enforcers. He was older than Kaela had expected, with silver hair and the kind of gentle features that belonged on a beloved grandfather. Only his eyes betrayed the steel beneath—cold, calculating, and utterly without mercy.

"Kaela Veyne," he said pleasantly, as if they were meeting at a garden party. "How good of you to finally accept our invitation."

"This wasn't an invitation," Kaela replied, hands moving instinctively toward her flames. "This was trespassing."

"Was it? I prefer to think of it as a job interview." Mirren gestured to the weapons around them. "You've seen what we're capable of. You've witnessed the consequences of defying the natural order. Surely a girl of your intelligence can appreciate the futility of continued resistance."

Through their bond, Kaela felt Ashfang's growing tension. Something was wrong here—more wrong than just being caught in the Council's most secret vault.

"The natural order," she repeated. "You mean the order you created by torturing spirits into submission."

"I mean the order that has kept humanity safe for five centuries," Mirren corrected, his voice hardening slightly. "Do you know what the world was like before the Sundering? Chaos. Eidolons running wild, answering to no authority but their own whims. Humans reduced to passengers in their own bodies."

"That's not—"

"True? How would you know? You've been listening to the propaganda of exiles and outcasts, people who have every reason to lie about our history." Mirren moved toward the Master Seal, his hand hovering over its crystalline surface. "But you could learn the truth. You could see what really happened."

Kaela felt a chill that had nothing to do with the vault's temperature. "What are you talking about?"

"A demonstration." Mirren's hand closed around the Master Seal, and immediately the chamber filled with silver light. "Your bond with your demon is strong—stronger than most. But every bond can be broken if you apply the right pressure in the right place."

The Seal's light reached toward Ashfang like grasping fingers, and where it touched him, his substance began to fade. Not disappearing—unraveling, being slowly torn apart at the fundamental level that defined his existence.

"Stop!" Kaela threw herself between the Seal and her demon, but the light passed through her as if she were made of mist. "You're killing him!"

"I'm showing you what he really is," Mirren said calmly. "A fragment of a broken spirit, held together by nothing more than your own desperate need to be special. Watch what happens when that illusion is stripped away."

The pain hit Kaela like a physical blow—not her own pain, but Ashfang's, transmitted through their bond with perfect clarity. She felt his essence being peeled away layer by layer, felt the memories and personality that made him who he was being systematically destroyed.

But she also felt something else. Love. Fierce, protective, unconditional love—not romantic, but something deeper. The love of two souls who had chosen each other against all odds and refused to let anything tear them apart.

"No," she said, her voice growing stronger. "You're wrong about everything."

Fire erupted from her hands—not the controlled flames she'd been practicing, but something primal and absolute. It struck the Master Seal's light and didn't burn it away—it absorbed it, transformed it, made it into something new.

"Impossible," Mirren breathed, his confident facade cracking for the first time. "The Seal can't be resisted. It's powered by the original Sundering ritual—"

"The original ritual that split unwilling spirits through force and trauma," Kaela interrupted, her flames growing brighter. "But our bond isn't based on force. It's based on choice. On trust. On love."

The silver light began to change, shot through with veins of ember-red that spread like cracks in glass. Where her fire touched the Seal's magic, it didn't destroy—it healed. It made whole.

"Ashfang," she called without taking her eyes off Mirren. "Are you still with me?"

"Always," came the reply, stronger than it had been moments before. "Though I have to say, your timing could use work."

The Master Seal's light flickered and died, its crystal surface now shot through with hairline fractures. Mirren stared at it in horror, then turned to his enforcers.

"Kill them," he ordered. "Both of them. Now."

The Guardian-bonded guards moved with professional efficiency, their spirits—a crystal hart and an ember hawk—flanking them with predatory grace. But they'd made a critical error in judgment.

They'd assumed that demon-bonded fighters would be undisciplined, relying on raw power rather than tactics. What they encountered instead was a partnership that had been forged in exile, tempered by constant danger, and strengthened by absolute trust.

Kaela's fire and Ashfang's shadows moved together like dance partners, each anticipating the other's needs. When the crystal hart charged, Ashfang's darkness blinded it while Kaela's flames forced it to stumble. When the ember hawk dove from above, Kaela's precise bursts drove it into the path of Ashfang's claws.

It was over in thirty seconds.

"Magnificent," Mirren said softly, seemingly unaware that his guards lay unconscious at his feet. "Do you see now? This is what the Eidolons were capable of. This perfect synthesis of light and shadow, order and chaos. And this is why they had to be stopped."

"Because they were powerful?" Kaela asked, not lowering her flames.

"Because they were free." Mirren's mask of grandfatherly kindness had finally slipped entirely, revealing the fanatic beneath. "Power without submission is anarchy. Strength without hierarchy is chaos. The Eidolons answered to no one, followed no rules, acknowledged no authority higher than their own desires."

"And that scared you."

"It should scare everyone." Mirren gestured to the broken Seal. "You've just demonstrated exactly why. With power like that, what's to stop you from deciding that you know better than everyone else? What's to stop you from imposing your will on the weak and helpless?"

Kaela looked at the unconscious guards, at the vault full of torture devices, at the man who had built his entire worldview on the premise that freedom was too dangerous to allow.

"Conscience," she said simply. "Empathy. Love. The things you've spent five centuries trying to eliminate because they're inconvenient to your vision of perfect order."

She walked to the Master Seal and placed her hands on its fractured surface. The crystal was warm to the touch, still humming with residual power from the broken ritual.

"This ends now," she said. "No more prisons. No more forced severances. No more torture in the name of purity."

Fire flowed from her hands into the Seal's crystal matrix, following the fracture lines she'd created. But instead of destroying it, she was transforming it—turning a weapon of separation into something that could reunite what had been torn apart.

"You don't understand what you're doing," Mirren warned. "If you restore the Eidolons, if you give spirits that kind of power again—"

"Then we'll deal with the consequences," Kaela interrupted. "Together. As equals. The way it should have been from the beginning."

The Master Seal cracked apart in her hands, its fragments turning to dust that glowed like stars before fading away. In the vault around them, the torture devices began to rust and corrode, their power sources severed.

"It's done," she said, feeling lighter than she had in months. "The old magic is broken."

"For now," Mirren said, his voice filled with quiet menace. "But there are other Seals, other weapons. You've won a battle, child, but the war is far from over."

He gestured, and a wall of brilliant white light surrounded him. When it faded, he was gone, leaving only the scent of ozone and the echo of distant laughter.

"Well," Ashfang said after the silence stretched too long, "that was appropriately dramatic."

"Too dramatic," Dax agreed, stepping over the unconscious guards. "He let us destroy the Seal too easily. Either he's not as smart as I thought, or—"

"Or he wanted us to destroy it," Kaela finished, the implications hitting her like cold water. "Because breaking one Seal does something that helps his larger plan."

They looked at each other in the flickering light of the vault's torches, each coming to the same uncomfortable conclusion.

"We need to get back to camp," Kaela said. "Fast. If Mirren wanted us to break the Seal, it means he's planning something bigger. Something that requires the old magic to be disrupted."

As they fled through the Citadel's foundations, carrying the unconscious guards' weapons and whatever intelligence they could gather, Kaela felt a growing sense of urgency. They'd won this encounter, but at what cost? And what had they just made possible by playing into the Council's hands?

One thing was certain: the war between light and shadow was about to escalate in ways none of them had anticipated.

And Kaela was starting to suspect that everything they thought they knew about the conflict was about to change.

Chapter 13: The Liberation

The war council convened not in a tent, but in the cramped, musty cellar of one of Kade Thistle's safe houses in the city's underbelly. The air was thick with the smell of damp earth and conspiracy. On a makeshift table, the stolen guard logbook lay open next to a crudely drawn map of the Citadel's lower levels.

"It's a suicide mission," Kade said, running a hand through his already frazzled hair. His usual nervousness was amplified to a near-fever pitch. "Fifty prisoners, most of them half-dead. You'll never get them out without the entire guard force coming down on you."

"That's why we don't let them," Kaela replied, her finger tracing a path on the map. "The logbook gives us a window. At the fourth bell of the morning watch, the night patrol ends and the day patrol begins. For seventeen minutes, guard presence on the prison level is at its absolute minimum—just two sentries at the main stairwell."

"Seventeen minutes isn't enough time to walk fifty people through a maze," Dax countered, her arms crossed. Mireclaw shifted on her shoulders, its head swaying as if scanning the cellar for threats.

"It is if the path is already clear and the transportation is waiting," Kaela said, looking at Kade.

Kade flinched under her gaze. "Getting two heavy transport wagons into the Citadel's service entrance without arousing suspicion is... difficult."

"But not impossible for your network," Kaela pressed. "You have contacts with the provisioners, the ones who bring in food and supplies. Your drivers go in posing as a late-night grain delivery. They wait at the service bay on sub-level two for precisely ten minutes. If we're not there, they leave."

The plan was audacious, relying on split-second timing and the flawless coordination of three separate teams.

"Team Alpha is us," Kaela explained, pointing to herself and Dax. "Infiltration. We go in through the storm drains, get to the prison level, and open the cells. Team Beta," she looked to a pair of veteran exiles, "you create a diversion. A fire at the West Barracks stables. Small enough to be contained, but big enough to draw the main guard force away from the Citadel's core."

"And Team Gamma is me," Kade finished, his voice grim. "The extraction. My people get the wagons in place and get the prisoners out of the city before the gates are sealed."

"Ember will be with the extraction team," Kaela added. "Ready for immediate triage. We have to assume the prisoners will be in no condition to help themselves."

The silence that followed was heavy with unspoken fears. Every part of the plan was a potential point of catastrophic failure.

Three nights later, Kaela and Dax moved like specters through the Citadel's storm drains. The diversion team had done their job perfectly; the distant clang of alarm bells and panicked shouts from the West Barracks told them that the Council's attention was focused elsewhere.

They reached the prison level five minutes before the fourth bell. As predicted, only two guards stood watch at the stairwell, their posture relaxed, their conversation lazy. Ashfang's shadows flowed from Kaela's feet, engulfing the guards before they could make a sound. They were bound and gagged in seconds, their unconscious forms hidden in a storage alcove.

"The clock is ticking," Ashfang's voice echoed in her mind.

Dax's lockpicks made quick, clicking sounds in the oppressive silence. The first cell door swung open. The young man inside didn't even look up, his eyes vacant, his demon spirit a barely visible wisp of shadow at his side.

"He can't walk," Dax whispered, her voice tight with fury.

It was the same in cell after cell. The prisoners were broken. Some were catatonic from forced severance; others were delirious with pain from failed "treatments." They were a collection of ghosts, their spiritual light dimmed to a flicker.

"We can't carry them all," Dax hissed as the fourth bell began its slow, tolling count. "We're out of time."

"We're not leaving them." Kaela's voice was steel. She moved to the first cell, kneeling in front of the vacant-eyed young man. Instead of trying to lift him, she reached out with her senses, finding the frayed edges of his bond.

We're getting you out, she sent, not with words, but with pure intent. *You are not forgotten.*

A flicker of light returned to the young man's eyes. He struggled to his feet, leaning on the wall for support.

It was agonizingly slow. Moving down the corridor, Kaela and Dax acted as spiritual anchors, offering sparks of their own strength to reignite the prisoners' will to move. They had to support the weakest, guiding the dazed, practically dragging the unconscious. The seventeen-minute window came and went. They were living on borrowed time.

Suddenly, Mireclaw hissed, its forked tongue tasting the air. "Patrol," Dax breathed. "Coming fast."

They were still two corridors away from the service bay. They could hear the rhythmic tramp of armored boots approaching.

"No more stealth," Kaela decided. She turned to the handful of prisoners who were lucid enough to understand. "Those who can fight, get ready. For the rest of you, don't stop moving."

When the patrol of six guards rounded the corner, they weren't met by helpless fugitives. They were met by a wall of desperate, defiant power. Kaela's fire erupted in a controlled wave, forcing them back. Dax's blade was a blur, disarming two guards before they could raise their weapons. The prisoners who could still summon their spirits fought with the ferocity of cornered animals.

The fight was brutal and blessedly short. As the last guard fell, the main Citadel alarm began to shriek— a piercing, continuous wail that meant the entire fortress was now on high alert.

"Go!" Kaela screamed.

They half-ran, half-stumbled the rest of the way, the alarms echoing in their ears. They burst into the service bay to see two large wagons, their canvas tops pulled back, and Kade's drivers looking terrified.

"We're out of time!" one of the drivers yelled. "They're sealing the gates!"

What followed was organized chaos. They lifted, pushed, and threw the prisoners into the backs of the wagons. Ember was already there, directing the placement of the most critically injured, her healing rain beginning to fall.

The wagons lurched into motion just as the first squad of Citadel Hunters stormed into the service bay. Ashfang roared, spewing a torrent of shadow and flame that engulfed the entrance, buying them precious seconds.

Kaela and Dax leaped onto the back of the last wagon as it sped out into the pre-dawn streets of Calyss. Behind them, the Citadel was a hornet's nest they had just kicked. Ahead of them lay the challenge of getting fifty wounded, traumatized people to safety in a city that was about to become a warzone.

They had done the impossible. They had liberated the Council's victims from the heart of its power. But as she looked at the dazed faces of the rescued, Kaela knew this wasn't an ending. It was the beginning of a battle for the soul of the city itself.

Chapter 14: Street War

The uprising began at dawn, and by midday, Calyss was burning.

Not literally—Kaela had learned enough about controlled fire to avoid that particular disaster. But metaphorically, the city was ablaze with the kind of civil unrest that happened when too many people discovered they'd been lied to for too long.

"Status report," she called to Dax, who was crouched behind an overturned market cart with Mireclaw coiled defensively around her shoulders.

"North square is secure—the rescued prisoners are safe with Ember's medical team," Dax replied, ducking as a Guardian-launched spear of light sizzled overhead. "East gate is still contested, and the Council's sending reinforcements from the Citadel."

Kaela nodded, trying to process tactical information while simultaneously coordinating the defense of three different positions. When they'd planned the prison break, none of them had anticipated it would spark a city-wide revolt. But apparently, seeing fifty broken teenagers liberated from secret dungeons had a way of making people question what else their government might be hiding.

"Ashfang, what's the situation at the fountain?"

Her demon materialized from the shadows between two burning Guardian banners, his obsidian scales reflecting the chaotic light of battle. "Twenty Council enforcers with full Guardian support, but they're having trouble advancing. Turns out citizens with improvised weapons are surprisingly motivated when they discover their children have been disappearing into torture chambers."

It was true. The rescue mission had succeeded beyond their wildest expectations—not just in freeing the prisoners, but in providing undeniable proof of the Council's crimes. When Ember's healers had begun treating the victims in full view of the morning market crowds, the city's carefully maintained order had simply... collapsed.

"Movement from the Citadel," called one of the Shadebond scouts, pointing toward the gleaming towers that dominated Calyss's skyline. "Looks like... oh, that's not good."

Kaela followed his gaze and felt her stomach drop. Marching from the Citadel in perfect formation was a company of Hunters—not the small patrol groups they'd been evading in the Wilds, but a full military unit with Guardian spirits that blazed like miniature suns.

"How many?" she asked, though she was afraid she already knew.

"Two hundred, maybe more. And they're not carrying sealing spears this time." The scout's voice was grim. "Those are killing weapons."

The crowd of revolutionaries around them—a mixture of demon-bonded exiles, sympathetic citizens, and people who were just angry enough to throw rocks at authority—suddenly seemed very small and very vulnerable.

"We need to fall back," Dax said urgently. "Get everyone to the safe houses and wait for—"

"No." Kaela's voice carried across the square with surprising authority. "We don't run. Not anymore."

"Kaela, there are two hundred of them and maybe fifty of us. The math is not encouraging."

"The math assumes this is about individual combat strength," Kaela replied, her mind racing through possibilities. "But it's not. This is about what we represent versus what they represent."

She climbed onto the overturned cart, making herself visible to both her allies and the approaching Hunter formation. "Listen to me," she called, her voice carrying over the sounds of distant fighting. "The Council is sending soldiers to restore order. They want to put the prisoners back in their cells, return the city to its comfortable lies, and pretend this morning never happened."

A murmur ran through the crowd—part fear, part anger, part desperate hope.

"But we're not going to let them," Kaela continued, fire beginning to dance around her hands. "Not because we're stronger than they are, but because we're fighting for something better. They fight to maintain a system built on fear and separation. We fight to prove that light and shadow can work together."

"Pretty speech," Dax muttered. "But speeches don't stop Guardian fire."

"No, they don't. But this might." Kaela gestured, and Ashfang flowed up beside her, his shadows intertwining with her flames in patterns that made the watching crowd gasp. "Balance tactics. We don't meet force with force—we meet rigidity with adaptation."

The Hunter formation was close enough now that she could see individual faces—professional soldiers who'd spent their lives training to fight demon-bonded "monsters." They advanced with textbook precision, Guardian spirits providing overlapping fields of protective light.

It was exactly the kind of disciplined, overwhelming assault that had crushed rebel movements for centuries.

It was also exactly the kind of approach that Kaela had learned to counter during her weeks of training with the Shadebond camp.

"Scatter formation," she called to her allies. "No battle lines, no concentrated targets. Make them fight fifty individual skirmishes instead of one big battle."

The demon-bonded fighters melted away from the square's center, taking positions on rooftops, in alleyways, behind market stalls. The watching citizens followed their lead, creating a fluid, unpredictable battlefield that the Hunters' rigid tactics weren't designed to handle.

"Fire support on my signal," Kaela continued, her voice somehow carrying to every fighter despite the chaos. "Not to kill—to confuse. Light and shadow, working together."

The first Hunter charge hit empty air. Their formation, perfect for advancing across open ground, became a liability when their targets refused to stand still and fight fair. Guardian spirits that had trained to counter demon fire found themselves facing coordinated attacks from multiple directions—shadows that blinded them while flames forced them to stumble, precise strikes that disrupted their formation without giving them clear targets for retaliation.

"Impossible," she heard one of the Hunter captains shouting. "Demons don't coordinate like this! They're supposed to be chaotic, undisciplined—"

"They're not just demons," Kaela called back, leaping from rooftop to rooftop with Ashfang's help. "They're partners. And partners watch each other's backs."

What followed wasn't really a battle in any traditional sense. It was more like a deadly game of tag played across the entire merchant district, with the Hunters trying to establish control while the revolutionaries demonstrated that control was an illusion when your opponents refused to be controlled.

Guardian fire met demon shadow in spectacular displays that would have been beautiful if they weren't potentially lethal. Citizens with no magical training found themselves running messages between combat zones, providing cover for wounded fighters, and generally proving that courage didn't require supernatural powers.

But the most important part of the fight wasn't the magic or the tactics—it was the audience.

Word of the uprising had spread throughout Calyss, and people were watching from windows, from distant rooftops, from anywhere they could get a clear view of the conflict. They were seeing demon-bonded fighters protecting civilians instead of threatening them. They were seeing cooperation instead of chaos. They were seeing proof that everything the Council had taught them about spirits and bonds and the necessity of rigid separation was simply wrong.

"They're not monsters," Kaela heard someone whisper from a nearby window. "They're just... people." That was the moment she knew they'd won.

Not the battle—that would continue for hours, with advances and retreats and small victories on both sides. But the war for hearts and minds, the struggle to prove that demon-bonded people deserved to exist as they were rather than be "fixed" or eliminated.

The Hunters could restore order to the streets, could drive the revolutionaries back into hiding, could even capture or kill some of them. But they couldn't unsee what the watching citizens had seen, couldn't unlearn the lesson that light and shadow were stronger together than apart.

"Fall back to secondary positions," Kaela called as the Hunter formation finally managed to adapt their tactics to the unconventional battlefield. "We've made our point."

As they retreated through the maze of Calyss's back streets, carrying their wounded and covering each other's escape, Kaela felt something she hadn't expected: satisfaction. Not victory—this was just one engagement in a longer war. But the satisfaction of knowing they'd changed something fundamental about how people thought about the conflict.

"That was either brilliant or insane," Dax panted as they reached the safe house where Ember's medical team was treating the rescued prisoners.

"Why not both?" Ashfang replied, settling into his usual position of protective watchfulness. "Though I have to admit, watching Guardian formation tactics fall apart in real time was deeply satisfying."

Kaela looked around the safe house at the mixture of demon-bonded fighters, rescued prisoners, and ordinary citizens who'd chosen to risk everything for the chance at something better. They were bruised, exhausted, and probably facing retaliation that would make today's battle look like a friendly disagreement.

But they were also united in a way that the Council's rigid hierarchy could never match. United by choice rather than compulsion, by shared purpose rather than shared fear. "What happens now?" asked one of the rescued prisoners, a girl whose demon bond had been partially severed but was slowly healing under Ember's care.

"Now we show them that today wasn't a fluke," Kaela said. "We prove that balance works, that cooperation is stronger than control, that people don't need to be forced into perfect little boxes to live together peacefully."

"And if the Council escalates?"

Kaela looked out the window toward the Citadel, where she could see Guardian lights gathering like storm clouds. Councilor Mirren would be planning his response, mobilizing resources, preparing for a conflict that would make today's street fighting look like a minor disagreement.

"Then we escalate too," she said quietly. "But we do it our way. Together."

As they retreated through the maze of Calyss's back streets, carrying their wounded and covering each other's escape, Kaela felt something she hadn't expected: satisfaction. Not victory, this was just one engagement in a longer war. But the satisfaction of knowing they'd changed something fundamental about how people thought about the conflict.

They regrouped in the cavernous cellar of a sympathetic baker, the air thick with the scent of yeast and healing herbs as Ember's team tended to the wounded. "We can't hold the streets," Dax reported, cleaning blood from her blade. "But we didn't have to. The city saw. That's a victory the Hunters can't take back."

Before Kaela could respond, one of Kade's scouts slipped into the cellar, breathless and wide-eyed. "Word from my contact inside the Citadel," the scout panted. "The uprising has thrown the Council into chaos. They're turning on each other, blaming everyone for the security failure. Councilor Mirren has called an emergency session, effective immediately, to consolidate power and decide on a final response."

A new kind of silence fell over the room. This was an opportunity they hadn't anticipated. "They'll be distracted," Ashfang's voice whispered in her mind. "Focused on internal politics, not external threats."

Kaela looked at the crude map of the Citadel they still had from their previous missions. An emergency session meant the Councilors would be gathered in one place, their plans laid bare for anyone who could get close enough to listen.

"They think we're scattered and hiding," Kaela said, a new, audacious plan forming in her mind. "They won't be expecting another infiltration. Not now." "You can't be serious," one of the exiles protested. "We just got out of there."

"We have to know what they're planning," Kaela insisted, her gaze locking with Dax's. "Winning a street fight means nothing if they're about to unleash something worse. I'm going in." This time, no one argued. They had fought a battle for the city's streets; now, Kaela would fight one for its future.

Chapter 15: Mirren Exposed

The Council of Light convened in emergency session three days after the uprising, and for the first time in five centuries, the chamber's perfect order showed cracks.

Kaela crouched in the ventilation shaft above the meeting hall, watching the most powerful people in Calyss argue with barely controlled fury. The infiltration had been risky—suicidal, according to Dax—but they needed to understand the Council's response to the revolution. More importantly, they needed evidence that would prove the systematic nature of the Council's crimes.

"Order!" Councilor Mirren's voice cut through the cacophony like a blade. "We will have order in this chamber, just as we will restore order to our city."

The other Councilors settled into uneasy silence, their Guardian spirits clustering around them like living shields. But Kaela could see the tension in their postures, the way their hands moved instinctively toward weapons that weren't there.

"The situation is contained," Mirren continued, his grandfatherly facade firmly in place despite the chaos of recent days. "A handful of demon-bonded terrorists managed to cause significant disruption, but their support among the general population remains minimal."

"Minimal?" Councilor Thorne's voice cracked with stress. "Half the merchant district is openly sympathetic to their cause! Our own citizens are questioning the necessity of exile laws!"

"Citizens are easily misled," Mirren replied smoothly. "They saw injured children and assumed malice where none existed. Our remedial treatment programs were designed to help those unfortunate souls, not harm them."

Kaela felt her hands clench into fists. Even now, even after everything that had been exposed, he was maintaining the lie that torture was therapy.

"Perhaps," suggested Councilor Brightwind, "we should consider... adjusting... our approach to demon-bonded individuals. The public response suggests our current methods may be creating more problems than they solve."

The temperature in the chamber seemed to drop several degrees. Mirren's gentle expression never wavered, but something cold and dangerous flickered behind his eyes.

"Are you suggesting, dear colleague, that five centuries of proven doctrine should be abandoned because of a single week of terrorist propaganda?"

"I'm suggesting that public order depends on public consent," Brightwind replied with obvious discomfort. "And consent requires trust. The revelations about our containment facilities have damaged that trust significantly."

"Then we rebuild trust by demonstrating strength," Mirren said. "By showing the citizenry what happens when order is challenged, when the natural hierarchy is disrupted."

He gestured, and the chamber's ceremonial braziers flared to life with brilliant white flame. But there was something wrong with the light—it was too pure, too perfect, lacking the natural flicker and warmth of ordinary fire.

"The Great Seal has served us well for five centuries," Mirren continued, his voice taking on the cadence of formal ritual. "But perhaps the time has come to implement the Final Solution."

Several Councilors shifted uncomfortably. Clearly, this was the first they'd heard of any "Final Solution."

"Councilor Mirren," Thorne said carefully, "what exactly are you proposing?"

"Complete separation," Mirren replied, his hands weaving patterns in the air that made the white flames dance. "Not just the containment of demon spirits, but their absolute elimination. A world cleansed of shadow, purified of corruption, perfected in light."

Kaela felt ice form in her stomach. Through their bond, she sensed Ashfang's growing alarm. This wasn't just authoritarian overreach—this was genocide.

"The logistics alone—" Brightwind began.

"Are already in place," Mirren interrupted. "The broken Master Seal served its purpose perfectly. Its destruction has destabilized the barriers between light and shadow, making all demon spirits vulnerable to mass targeting."

The pieces clicked together in Kaela's mind with horrible clarity. Mirren had wanted them to break the Seal. He'd manipulated the entire confrontation, knowing that destroying the ancient artifact would create the very vulnerability he needed for his final plan.

"You're talking about killing thousands of innocent spirits," Councilor Thorne said, his face pale with horror. "Many of them bonded to children who had no choice in the matter."

"I'm talking about completing the work our predecessors began," Mirren replied calmly. "The Great Sundering was a half-measure, born of squeamishness and sentiment. We separated light from shadow but allowed the shadow to persist. That was our mistake."

He raised his hands, and the white flames responded, growing brighter and more intense. But as the light reached its peak, something impossible happened.

Shadow erupted from Mirren's own silhouette.

Not ordinary darkness—this was living shadow, writhing and coiling with obvious intelligence. It flowed around the chamber like spilled ink, and where it touched the white flames, both light and dark began to... merge.

"Impossible," Brightwind whispered. "You're... you're dual-bonded."

Mirren's mask of grandfatherly kindness finally slipped completely, revealing the fanatic beneath. "I am whole," he said, his voice carrying harmonics that belonged to both light and shadow. "I am what humanity was meant to be before weakness and fear drove us to mutilate our own souls."

Above him, two spirits materialized—one a magnificent unicorn whose horn blazed with purifying light, the other a seraph whose wings dripped with corrupted radiance. They moved together with perfect synchronization, light and shadow aspects of what had once been a single, complete Eidolon.

"For five centuries," Mirren continued, "I have maintained this bond in secret, studying the true nature of spiritual integration while teaching others to fear it. I have experienced the power of wholeness while preaching the necessity of division."

"You're a hypocrite," Thorne accused, backing away from the writhing shadows. "Everything you've taught us, everything we've built—it's all based on lies."

"It's based on necessity," Mirren corrected. "The common people cannot handle the responsibility of true power. They would use integration for petty purposes, personal gain, individual satisfaction. Only through careful control, through the guidance of those wise enough to bear the burden of wholeness, can humanity achieve its true potential."

Kaela had heard enough. She kicked out the ventilation grate and dropped into the chamber, fire already blazing around her hands.

"The only thing you've achieved," she said, landing in a crouch beside the ceremonial braziers, "is proving that absolute power corrupts absolutely."

The Councilors scattered like startled birds, their Guardian spirits taking defensive positions. But Mirren simply smiled, his dual nature now revealed in its full, terrible glory.

"Kaela Veyne," he said warmly. "How good of you to join us. You're just in time to witness the birth of a new age."

"I'm just in time to stop a madman," she corrected, stepping forward as Ashfang materialized beside her. "You want to talk about true power? About what integration really means? Let me show you."

Fire and shadow flowed together around her, not in the harsh merger that Mirren displayed, but in a harmony born of trust, choice, and genuine partnership. Where his spirits moved with the mechanical precision of master and tool, hers danced with the fluid grace of equals.

"You call that integration?" Mirren laughed, his unicorn's horn beginning to glow with lethal intensity. "Child, you have no idea what true unity looks like."

"Actually," Kaela said, feeling the familiar calm that came before decisive action, "I think I do. The difference is, my unity is based on love, not control."

The battle that followed would be remembered in the histories as the moment the old order finally shattered. Light and shadow clashed in the Council chamber with forces that hadn't been seen since the Great Sundering, but this time, the conflict wasn't about separation—it was about what integration really meant.

Mirren fought with the overwhelming power of someone who had spent centuries accumulating magical strength. His attacks were precise, devastating, and backed by the kind of raw force that could level buildings.

But Kaela fought with something he couldn't understand: balance. Every flame she conjured was matched by Ashfang's shadows. Every assault they weathered was turned into an opportunity for counterattack. They moved as one being, their bond so seamless that it was impossible to tell where one ended and the other began.

"Impossible," Mirren snarled as his perfect formations were disrupted by their fluid tactics. "You're just a child! I have centuries of experience, the wisdom of ages—"

"You have power," Kaela interrupted, weaving between his attacks with Ashfang's help. "But you don't have understanding. You forced your spirits together through domination and called it unity. But real integration comes from choice, from trust, from love."

As if to prove her point, she reached out through her bond with Ashfang, not to command or control, but to ask. Their essences flowed together briefly—not the permanent fusion that created Eidolons, but a momentary sharing that multiplied their strength without diminishing their individuality.

The resulting strike shattered Mirren's defenses and sent him sprawling across the chamber floor. His dual spirits flickered and wavered, their forced unity beginning to unravel under the stress of combat.

"You see?" Kaela said, standing over the fallen Councilor. "That's the difference between us. You think power means control. I know it means cooperation."

Around the chamber, the remaining Councilors watched in stunned silence as five centuries of absolute authority crumbled before their eyes. Their leader, the man who had embodied their ideals of purity and order, was revealed as the greatest hypocrite of all—someone who had forbidden others to seek the very wholeness he had claimed for himself.

"It's over," Kaela said, addressing the chamber. "The lies, the torture, the systematic oppression of people whose only crime was being inconvenient to your vision of perfection. All of it ends now."

"You think exposing me changes anything?" Mirren gasped from the floor, his spirits beginning to separate as his forced bond weakened. "The system is bigger than one man. The fears that created it run deeper than rational thought. Even if you destroy me, someone else will take my place."

"Maybe," Kaela acknowledged. "But they'll do it in a world where people have seen what's possible when light and shadow work together instead of fighting each other. That changes everything."

As Council guards finally arrived to restore order to their shattered chamber, Kaela and Ashfang melted back into the shadows, their mission complete. They had the evidence they needed—not just documents or testimony, but living proof that the Council's entire philosophy was built on hypocrisy and lies.

Mirren's exposure would ripple through Calyss like wildfire, sparking conversations and questions that had been suppressed for centuries. The revolution had gained something more valuable than territory or resources—it had gained legitimacy.

"Well," Ashfang said as they made their escape through the city's rooftops, "that was dramatically satisfying."

"Dramatically effective," Kaela corrected. "Now everyone knows that the man who preached separation was secretly practicing integration. Kind of undermines the whole 'demons are inherently corrupting' argument."

"What happens next?"

Kaela looked out over Calyss, where citizens were already gathering in the squares to discuss what they'd learned. The old order was crumbling, but what would replace it was still being decided by thousands of individual choices, millions of small acts of courage or cowardice.

"Next," she said, "we prove that we can build something better than what we're tearing down."

The hardest part of any revolution, she was learning, wasn't winning the battles—it was deciding what came after the victory.

Chapter 16: The Great Seal Stirs

The first sign something was wrong came at dawn, when every demon in the Shadebond camp began screaming at once.

Kaela jolted awake to the sound of spiritual agony—not physical pain, but something deeper, more fundamental. Through her bond with Ashfang, a nauseating, spiritual vertigo, a pulling sensation that came with a headache that pulsed in time with the Seal's unseen energy. It was a constant, low-grade agony designed to unmake them from the inside out.

"What's happening?" she gasped, rolling out of her bedroll as Ashfang materialized beside her, his form flickering like a candle in wind.

"The Great Seal," he managed through gritted teeth. "It's... active. Actually active, for the first time since the Sundering."

Around the camp, chaos reigned. Demons pressed close to their bonded partners, seeking comfort and protection from whatever force was trying to tear them away. The humans weren't much better—the spiritual drain was affecting them too, leaving them dizzy, nauseous, and profoundly afraid.

"Ember!" Kaela called, stumbling toward the healer's tent. "We need answers!"

She found Ember hunched over Thyriel, her storm owl's feathers dulled to gray and her breathing labored. The usually composed healer looked up with eyes wide with terror.

"It's the original Seal," Ember said, her voice barely above a whisper. "The one they used for the Great Sundering. Mirren must have found a way to reactivate it."

"To do what?"

"To finish what the Council started five centuries ago." Dax appeared in the tent entrance, supporting Mireclaw, whose usual vibrant green had faded to sickly yellow. "Mass severance. Every demon bond in the world, cut simultaneously."

The implications hit Kaela like a physical blow. Not just exile or imprisonment—complete elimination of every shadow spirit on the continent. Thousands of demons, hundreds of bonded partners, all of them dying in an instant of magical genocide.

"How long do we have?" she asked, though she wasn't sure she wanted to know the answer.

"Hours, maybe," Ashfang replied, his form solidifying as he fought against the Seal's pull. "The ritual takes time to build to full power. But once it reaches critical threshold..."

He didn't need to finish. They all understood what would happen when the Great Seal reached full activation.

"Then we stop it," Kaela said with more confidence than she felt. "We find the Seal and break it before Mirren can complete his ritual."

"Find it?" Dax laughed bitterly. "Kaela, the Great Seal isn't a weapon you can pick up and smash. It's a magical construct the size of a city district, built into the foundation of reality itself. The Abyssal Rift—the scar left by the original Sundering—that's where it's anchored."

"Then we go to the Rift."

"It's three days' travel through hostile territory, assuming we could even make it past the Council's defensive lines. And that's if our demons don't get ripped away from us en route. But its control mechanism, the Ritual Focus that allows it to be aimed and fired, has always been housed here in Calyss, deep within the Citadel. Mirren doesn't need to be at the Rift to pull the trigger; he just needs to be at the controls."

Kaela looked around the tent at her friends, her chosen family, all of them facing extinction because one madman couldn't tolerate the existence of people he couldn't control. The old familiar rage began to build in her chest—not the wild, destructive fury of her early days, but something focused and purposeful.

"Then we don't go around the defenses," she said. "We go through them."

Within an hour, every demon-bonded fighter in the camp was armed and moving. Not toward the Abyssal Rift—that would come later—but toward Calyss itself. If Mirren was powering the Great Seal from the Citadel's ritual chambers, they needed to disrupt his control before the Seal reached full activation.

It was a desperate plan, bordering on suicidal. They would be attacking the most heavily defended position in the kingdom with maybe sixty fighters, while their demons were being systematically weakened by the very weapon they were trying to stop.

But as they approached the city's outer walls, something unexpected happened.

The gates opened.

Not for them—for a stream of people flowing out of Calyss like water from a broken dam. Citizens carrying hastily packed belongings, families with children clutched close, merchants abandoning their shops to flee whatever was happening inside the city.

"Refugees," Dax observed. "Something's gone very wrong in there."

They intercepted a family of fleeing merchants, who told a story that made Kaela's blood run cold. The Council had declared martial law following Mirren's exposure, but instead of restoring order, the city had descended into chaos. Guardian-bonded enforcers were conducting house-to-house searches for "shadow sympathizers." Anyone who had shown support for the demon-bonded revolution was being arrested or simply disappearing.

And in the Citadel itself, strange lights had been seen dancing around the towers—not the warm golden glow of Guardian magic, but something harsh and white and hungry.

"He's not just targeting demons," Kaela realized. "He's targeting anyone who might oppose him. This isn't about purity—it's about absolute control."

"Which means we have allies inside the city," Ashfang pointed out, his form more stable now that they were closer to the source of the Seal's power. "People who are just as desperate to stop this as we are."

It was true. As they moved through Calyss's outer districts, they found pockets of resistance— Guardian-bonded citizens who had turned against the Council, ordinary people who had organized into makeshift militias, even some Council soldiers who had refused orders and gone into hiding.

The revolution that had started with a handful of demon-bonded exiles had become something much larger: a coalition of everyone who believed that diversity was stronger than uniformity, that cooperation was better than domination.

"The Citadel's sealed," reported one of the resistance leaders, a middle-aged woman whose crystal hart stood guard while she sketched tactical diagrams in the dirt. "Mirren's barricaded himself in the ritual chambers with his inner circle. But the Seal's power is affecting the whole city—Guardian spirits are getting weaker, magic is becoming unstable."

"Which gives us an opening," Kaela said, studying the woman's maps. "If Guardian magic is compromised, then their defensive advantages are neutralized."

"It also means our demons are fighting against the Seal's pull with every step we take toward the Citadel," Dax pointed out.

"Then we move fast."

The assault on the Citadel began at sunset, timed to coincide with the daily shift change when security would be momentarily disrupted. But as they approached the ancient fortress, it became clear that conventional tactics wouldn't work.

The building itself was changing.

Where once there had been clean white stone and elegant spires, now there were twisted growths of crystalline matter that pulsed with that harsh, hungry light. The very architecture was being transformed by the Seal's power, becoming something alien and wrong.

"It's not just a weapon," Ember breathed, staring up at the transformed structure. "It's alive. The Seal is actually alive."

Through their bond, Kaela felt Ashfang's revulsion and recognition. "You've seen this before," she said.

"During the original Sundering. This is what the Eidolons looked like when they were being torn apart—reality itself trying to reject what was being done to it." His voice carried five centuries of traumatic memory. "If Mirren completes the ritual, it won't just eliminate demons. It'll scar the world permanently."

The thought of that crystalline wrongness spreading across the continent, of magic itself being warped into a tool of oppression, gave Kaela the final push she needed.

"New plan," she announced to the assembled fighters. "We don't just stop the ritual. We reverse it."

"Reverse it how?" asked the resistance leader.

"The same way we've been fighting this whole time," Kaela replied, fire beginning to dance around her hands as she spoke. "Together. Light and shadow, Guardian and demon, working as partners instead of master and slave."

She looked up at the transformed Citadel, where Mirren was even now completing the preparations for magical genocide. Through the bond, she felt Ashfang's absolute trust, his willingness to follow her into whatever came next.

"If the Great Seal is designed to tear spirits apart," she continued, "then maybe what we need is enough unified spirits to tear the Seal apart instead."

It was audacious to the point of insanity. The kind of plan that required perfect coordination, absolute trust, and more than a little luck. But as she looked around at the faces surrounding her—demon-bonded exiles, Guardian-bonded rebels, ordinary citizens who had decided that freedom was worth fighting for—Kaela felt something she hadn't expected.

Hope.

They were going to storm a fortress that was being actively transformed by hostile magic, fight their way through whatever defenses Mirren had prepared, and somehow use the power of cooperation to unravel a spell that had shaped the world for five centuries.

It was impossible.

It was necessary.

And as the last light faded from the sky and the assault began, Kaela discovered that sometimes impossible and necessary were the same thing.

Chapter 17: Setbacks & Sacrifices

The first wave of the assault lasted exactly seventeen minutes before everything went wrong.

Kaela pressed herself against the crystalline wall of what had once been the Citadel's main courtyard, trying to catch her breath while chaos erupted around her. The plan had been solid—multiple entry points, coordinated strikes, overwhelming the transformed defenses before they could adapt.

The plan had also been based on the assumption that the defenders would be human.

"Fall back!" she heard Dax shouting from somewhere in the maze of twisted architecture. "The constructs are adapting!"

Constructs. That was the polite term for what the Great Seal had done to the Citadel's Guardian-bonded defenders. Kaela had seen three of them so far, and each one had been a fresh nightmare— human forms fused with their Guardian spirits into something that was neither fully alive nor completely dead. They moved with mechanical precision, fought without pain or fear, and seemed to grow stronger the longer the battle continued.

"Kaela!" Ember's voice, tight with strain. "We need fire support on the east wall!"

Kaela pushed away from her cover and sprinted across the courtyard, dodging crystalline spears that erupted from the ground with each step. The east wall was a disaster—half their fighters pinned down by a construct that had once been Captain Lyr, the elite Guardian duelist she'd heard about in camp stories.

Now Lyr was something else entirely. His form flickered between human and crystal stag, antlers of pure light sweeping in deadly arcs while his lower body had become a pillar of living stone. Where he stepped, the ground turned to the same hungry crystal that was consuming the Citadel.

"He's turning the battlefield," one of the resistance fighters gasped as Kaela slid into cover beside them. "Every surface he touches becomes part of the Seal's network."

Through her bond, Kaela felt Ashfang's grim assessment. The construct wasn't just fighting them—it was transforming the very space they fought in, making it increasingly hostile to demon-bonded spirits.

"Can we get around him?"

"Not without losing half our people. He's blocking the only access to the inner keep."

Kaela studied the situation, her mind racing through possibilities. They needed to neutralize the construct without getting close enough for it to transform them too. But conventional attacks weren't working—the thing absorbed Guardian fire and seemed immune to physical damage.

"Ashfang," she said quietly, "how do you feel about a distraction?"

"I feel like it's going to be dangerous, probably stupid, and almost certainly our only option," he replied, materializing beside her with shadows already wreathing his form. "What did you have in mind?"

Before she could answer, a scream echoed across the courtyard—not the battle cry of warriors in combat, but the sound of someone in absolute agony. Kaela turned to see one of the younger demon-bonded fighters being pulled apart by the Seal's power, his bond with his shadow-bat stretching like a rubber band about to snap.

"No!" The resistance leader—the woman with the crystal hart—threw herself toward the boy, but she was too far away.

That's when Ember did something that would haunt Kaela's dreams for the rest of her life.

The healer stepped directly into the Seal's energy field, placing herself between the destructive force and the failing bond. Thyriel spread her wings wide, her storm-spirit nature allowing her to absorb and redirect the magical assault.

For a moment, it worked. The boy's bond stabilized, his demon solidified, and it looked like Ember's intervention had saved them both.

Then the redirected energy found a new target.

Ember's scream was cut short as the Seal's power tore through her own bond, ripping Thyriel away

147

from her with violent finality. The storm owl's form scattered like mist in wind, and Ember collapsed to the crystalline ground, her eyes empty of everything that had made her who she was.

"EMBER!" Dax's roar of fury and grief cut through every other sound in the courtyard. Mireclaw's scales flared to venomous brilliance as the pair charged toward where their friend had fallen.

But the construct that had been Captain Lyr was already moving, drawn by the magical disruption. Its crystalline hooves rang against the transformed stone as it approached Ember's motionless form.

"Not happening," Kaela snarled, and for the first time since her early training, she let her control slip entirely.

Fire erupted from her in a torrent that turned the air itself into a weapon. Not the precise, disciplined flames she'd spent months learning to shape, but something primal and absolute—the rage of someone watching her family be destroyed by forces too vast to fight.

The construct staggered under the assault, its crystal form cracking as heat beyond its tolerances washed over it. But instead of falling, it began to change again, adapting to incorporate her flames into its own structure.

"It's learning!" someone shouted. "Every attack makes it stronger!"

That's when Kaela understood the true horror of what Mirren had created. The Great Seal wasn't just a weapon—it was a self-improving system that grew more powerful with each victory, more adaptable with each challenge. Every spirit it consumed made it hungrier. Every bond it severed made it more efficient at severing the next one.

"Fall back," she called, her voice cutting through the chaos. "Everyone fall back now!"

The retreat was a nightmare of running battles and desperate rear-guard actions. They lost three more fighters to the constructs' pursuit, including the boy Ember had died to save—his weakened bond finally snapping under the stress of combat.

By the time they reached the temporary safe zone they'd established in the ruins of a Guardian temple, their force had been cut in half. Worse, the survivors were showing signs of spiritual exhaustion—their bonds strained by proximity to the Seal's power, their demons flickering in and out of existence like candles in a hurricane.

"Status report," Kaela said, trying to project leadership while her heart felt like it was being torn apart.

"Fifteen confirmed dead," Dax reported, her voice hollow with grief. "Eight more missing, probably captured. The constructs have sealed off all approaches to the inner keep."

"And our demons are getting weaker by the hour," added one of the resistance fighters. "If we can't end this soon, the Seal will drain us all just through proximity."

Kaela looked around at the faces of her remaining allies—exhausted, grief-stricken, but still determined to fight. They'd lost friends, family, people who'd become irreplaceable parts of their found community. The easy camaraderie that had carried them through the earlier battles was gone, replaced by something harder and more desperate.

"Ember knew this might happen," she said quietly. "She knew that stopping the Seal would cost more than we wanted to pay. But she also knew that the alternative was worse."

"The alternative," Dax said bitterly, "wasn't watching our healer get torn apart because she tried to save someone who died anyway."

"No. The alternative was watching everyone get torn apart because we weren't brave enough to try."

Kaela stood up, feeling the weight of command settling around her shoulders like a cloak made of lead. Every decision from here on would cost lives. Every choice would require someone to sacrifice something irreplaceable.

"The constructs are adapting to our individual attacks," she continued. "But they're still operating on the Seal's base programming—separation, division, the breaking of bonds. What if we gave them something they couldn't break apart?"

"What do you mean?" asked one of the Guardian-bonded rebels.

"Mass coordination. Every spirit in perfect sync, every bond reinforcing every other bond." Kaela looked at the mixture of demon-bonded exiles and Guardian-bonded rebels around her. "Light and shadow working together so closely that the Seal can't tell where one ends and the other begins."

"That's... theoretically possible," admitted the resistance leader. "But the level of trust required, the precision of timing—one mistake and the backlash would kill everyone involved."

"Then we don't make mistakes."

Ashfang materialized beside her, his form more solid than it had been all day. "You're talking about fusion," he said. "Not permanent, but temporary merging of spirits across bond lines. It's been tried before."

"What happened?"

"Sometimes it worked. Sometimes it didn't. When it didn't work..." He paused, choosing his words carefully. "Let's just say that separation anxiety becomes a very literal problem."

Kaela looked at the faces around her—people who had already lost so much, who were being asked to risk everything on a plan that might kill them all. She thought about Ember's sacrifice, about the boy who'd died despite her intervention, about all the prisoners still held in the Citadel's transformed dungeons.

"I can't ask anyone else to take this risk," she said finally. "But I can't ask anyone to watch while the world gets torn apart either. Anyone who wants to try this with me, step forward. Anyone who doesn't, no judgment—you've already done more than enough."

Every single person in the circle stepped forward.

"Idiots," Dax said, but she was smiling through her tears. "We're all absolute idiots."

"Probably," Kaela agreed. "But we're idiots together. And sometimes that's enough."

As they began the delicate process of synchronizing their bonds, preparing for an assault that would either save the world or destroy them all, Kaela felt something she hadn't expected: peace.

Not the peace of victory—that was still uncertain. But the peace of knowing that whatever happened next, they would face it as a unified whole. Light and shadow, Guardian and demon, human and spirit, all of them choosing cooperation over domination.

Ember would have approved, she thought. And maybe, if they were very lucky and very good, her sacrifice would mean something more than just another casualty in an impossible war.

The final assault would begin at dawn. One way or another, this would all be over soon.

Chapter 18: Betrayal Revealed

The supply drop was supposed to arrive at midnight—medical supplies, food, and most importantly, the specialized crystals they needed to stabilize their bond-fusion attempt. When Kade Thistle's messenger arrived three hours late with empty hands and shifty eyes, Kaela knew something had gone very wrong.

"Where are the supplies?" she asked, studying the nervous young man who'd been part of Kade's spirit-trading network since the early days of the resistance.

"Delayed," he stammered, unable to meet her gaze. "Council patrols, you know. Had to take the long way around."

Through her bond with Ashfang, Kaela felt the familiar tingle of danger. Something in the messenger's voice, his posture, the way he kept glancing toward the ruined temple's entrance—it all spoke of deception poorly concealed.

"Where's Kade?" Dax asked, Mireclaw's scales shifting to warning colors around her shoulders.

"He'll be here soon. Had to... had to handle some last-minute negotiations."

Kaela exchanged a look with Dax. In the weeks since they'd been working with the spirit traders, Kade had never missed a personal delivery. He was too paranoid about Council infiltration to trust anyone else with sensitive cargo.

"What kind of negotiations?" Kaela pressed.

The messenger's composure finally cracked. "Look, you don't understand the position we're in. The Council's offering amnesty, real amnesty, for information about resistance operations. Clean slates, full pardons, protection for our families—"

"You sold us out," Dax said flatly.

"We sold out the location of one supply cache!" the messenger protested. "That's all! Kade said it was a reasonable loss to ensure our long-term survival—"

He never finished the sentence. Ashfang materialized behind him with predatory silence, shadows wrapping around the man's throat just tight enough to focus his attention.

"How long ago?" Kaela asked, her voice deadly calm.

"Two hours," the messenger gasped. "Maybe three. They should have hit the cache by now, but the main operation—"

"What main operation?"

"Tomorrow's assault. Kade knows about the bond-fusion plan. He knows about the timing, the location, everything." The man's face was pale with terror, but also with the relief of finally telling the truth. "They're going to be waiting for you."

The implications hit Kaela like cold water. Their desperate gamble wasn't just risky—it was a trap. Mirren would be prepared for exactly what they were planning, would have countermeasures in place, would probably turn their own coordination against them.

"How much does the Council know?" she asked.

"Everything Kade knew. Which is... most of it." The messenger's voice dropped to a whisper. "He's been feeding them information for weeks. Started small— supply routes, safe house locations. But after what happened to his nephew..."

"His nephew?" Dax's grip tightened on her blade.

"Captured during the first prison raid. Council's been holding him in the deep cells, using him as leverage. Kade tried to resist, but when they started sending him fingers..."

Kaela felt sick. Not just at the Council's cruelty, but at her own failure to see what was happening. She'd trusted Kade, relied on his network, built crucial plans around resources he'd promised to provide. And all the while, he'd been trapped in an impossible situation—forced to choose between the resistance and his family.

"Where is he now?" she asked.

"Meeting with his Council contact. Supposed to provide final details about your assault plan in exchange for his nephew's release."

"And you believe they'll actually release the boy?"

The messenger's bitter laugh told her everything she needed to know.

"Council doesn't release prisoners," Dax said grimly. "They just find new ways to use them."

Kaela closed her eyes, feeling the weight of another impossible decision settling on her shoulders. Kade's betrayal had compromised their entire operation, but it wasn't really betrayal—it was desperation. A man trying to save his family with the only currency the Council would accept.

"Where's the meeting?" she asked.

"The old amphitheater, in the ruins outside the city. But you can't—"

"Can't what? Stop him from destroying everything we've worked for?" Kaela's voice carried more exhaustion than anger. "He's not the villain here. But he's about to become one if we don't intervene."

"It's a trap," Ashfang pointed out. "The Council knows we know about the betrayal now. They'll be expecting us."

"Probably. But we can't let Kade complete that handover. And we can't abandon his nephew." Kaela looked around at her remaining allies—tired, grieving, facing impossible odds with every hour that passed. "How many more people are we going to lose to this system that turns love into a weapon?"

Dax was already checking her weapons. "How do you want to handle this?"

"Carefully. The Council's expecting desperate resistance fighters charging in to stop a betrayal. Let's give them something else instead."

The old amphitheater had been abandoned since before the Sundering—a relic of an age when humans and spirits gathered for celebrations rather than separations. Now it was a perfect meeting ground: isolated, defensible, with multiple escape routes for all parties involved.

Which made it an equally perfect place for an ambush.

Kaela and her team approached through the ruins with painstaking stealth, using Ashfang's shadow-walking to avoid the Council's perimeter guards. What they found in the amphitheater's central arena made her heart sink.

Kade Thistle knelt in the center of the ancient stone circle, his hands bound behind his back. Beside him was a boy of maybe fourteen—presumably his nephew—barely conscious and showing clear signs of long-term abuse. Around them stood a dozen Council Hunters with their Guardian spirits providing overlapping fields of protection.

And standing at the arena's edge, looking like a grandfather disappointed in his family's behavior, was Councilor Mirren himself.

"Kade Thistle," Mirren was saying, his voice carrying easily across the amphitheater. "You've provided valuable service to the Council, and for that you have our gratitude. But I'm afraid recent events have made your continued existence... problematic."

"You promised," Kade gasped, staring at his nephew's battered form. "You said if I gave you the resistance plans, you'd let him go."

"I said I'd release him," Mirren corrected gently. "I never specified in what condition. Death is a form of release, after all."

The casual cruelty of it made Kaela's hands clench into fists. This was what the Council's "order" really meant—a world where love was weakness to be exploited, where loyalty was a tool for manipulation, where mercy was something that happened to other people.

"However," Mirren continued, "I am not without compassion. Your nephew can live—in fact, he can be completely healed and returned to his family. All you need to do is perform one final service."

"What service?"

Mirren gestured, and one of the Hunters approached carrying a crystal rod that made Kaela's skin crawl just looking at it. "Call them. Call the resistance fighters you know are watching from the shadows. Convince them to surrender, and both you and your nephew walk away free."

"And if they don't surrender?"

"Then they die here, along with you and the boy. But at least their deaths will serve a purpose— demonstrating to the world what happens when order is challenged."

Kaela felt the trap closing around them. Mirren hadn't just bought Kade's information—he'd used it to set up this moment, this choice between saving two lives and sacrificing the resistance that could save thousands.

"Kaela," Ashfang whispered through their bond, "we should go. This isn't a rescue—it's bait."

He was right. The smart play was to retreat, regroup, find another way to stop the Great Seal. Kade had made his choice when he started feeding information to the Council. His nephew was a tragedy, but not one they could fix without destroying everything else they'd worked for.

But as she watched Kade struggle with the impossible decision Mirren had forced on him, Kaela realized something important: this was exactly the kind of thinking that had created the current crisis. The willingness to write off individuals for the greater good, to accept necessary sacrifices, to treat people as acceptable losses in service of some larger agenda.

"New plan," she whispered to her team.

"Please tell me it doesn't involve walking into an obvious trap," Dax replied.

"It involves walking into an obvious trap and turning it inside out."

Before anyone could stop her, Kaela stood up and walked into the amphitheater.

"Councilor Mirren," she called, her voice carrying across the ancient stones. "I hear you wanted to see me."

The Council forces immediately shifted into defensive positions, Guardian spirits blazing with protective light. But Mirren himself seemed more pleased than surprised.

"Kaela Veyne. How good of you to accept my invitation. Though I notice you came alone—how unlike you."

"Did I?" Kaela smiled, and around the amphitheater's rim, shadows began to move. Not just her own people, but dozens of figures emerging from concealment—Guardian-bonded rebels, ordinary citizens, even some Council soldiers who'd finally had enough of serving a system that thrived on suffering.

"You wanted a demonstration," Kaela continued, walking toward the center of the arena where Kade and his nephew waited. "Let me show you what real unity looks like."

What happened next would be remembered as the moment the revolution stopped being about demon-bonded people demanding their rights and became about everyone demanding their humanity back.

Light and shadow flowed together around the amphitheater as Guardian and demon spirits moved in perfect coordination. Not the forced harmony of Mirren's dual bond, but the chosen cooperation of people who had decided that separation was the enemy, not each other.

The Council Hunters found themselves surrounded not by chaotic rebels, but by a unified force that moved like a single organism. Every attack was anticipated, every defense was coordinated, every individual action served the collective purpose.

It was over in minutes.

As the last Hunter fell unconscious (they'd chosen capture over killing wherever possible), Kaela helped Kade to his feet and began working on his bonds.

"Why?" he asked, tears streaming down his face. "After what I did, why would you—"

"Because the Council turned your love into a weapon," Kaela replied, freeing his hands and moving to check on his nephew. "And because proving that love doesn't have to be weakness is the whole point of what we're doing."

Mirren, cornered but not yet defeated, raised his hands as his dual spirits began to manifest. "Touching," he said, his grandfatherly mask finally slipping completely. "But ultimately pointless. You've saved two lives at the cost of thousands. The Great Seal reaches full power at dawn, and nothing you've accomplished here will change that."

Before Captain Lyr's forces could close in, Mirren raised a hand that held a small, intricately carved piece of obsidian. He crushed it.

"This is not over, child," he hissed, as shadows erupted from the ground—not the living darkness of a demon, but a dead, light-devouring void. The shadows engulfed him completely. For a heartbeat, there was only a pillar of absolute blackness, and then it imploded, leaving behind only the scent of ozone and the faint echo of his laughter.

"Escape artifact," Dax swore, kicking at the spot where he'd vanished. "Pre-Sundering. He had this planned from the start."

Mirren was gone, but his threat remained, more potent than ever. He had what he wanted: the final details of their plan and the freedom to ensure it failed.

"You're right," Kaela agreed, helping the injured boy to his feet. "This doesn't stop the Seal. But it does prove something important."

"Which is?"

"That your way isn't the only way. That cooperation beats coercion. That people will choose to work together if you give them the chance." She looked around at the mixture of Guardian and demon-bonded fighters who had risked everything to save two people they'd never met. "And that makes all the difference."

As they evacuated the amphitheater, carrying the wounded and securing the captured Council forces, Kaela felt something shift in the spiritual atmosphere around them. The Great Seal was still building toward its climactic activation, still threatening to tear apart every demon bond in existence.

But for the first time since this all began, she felt like they might actually have a chance to stop it.

Not through individual heroics or overwhelming power, but through the collective strength of people who had chosen to trust each other.

It was going to be enough. It had to be.

Chapter 19: The Desperate Hope

The war council convened in the ruins of an ancient temple dedicated to forgotten gods, and for the first time in five centuries, Guardian and demon spirits shared the same sacred space without violence. The air was cold, thick with the metallic tang of fear and the low, oppressive hum of the Great Seal building towards its climax. It was a sound no one could hear with their ears, but every bonded person felt it in their soul... a relentless, grinding pressure that promised annihilation.

Kaela stood at the center of the gathering, a stolen map of the Citadel spread across a fallen altar stone. She looked out at the faces illuminated by the flickering torchlight, a mosaic of their unlikely coalition. Demon-bonded exiles with their wild, intelligent spirits sat beside stone-faced Guardian-bonded rebels whose partners pulsed with disciplined light. Council defectors, their fine robes now tattered and stained, shared tactical information with spirit traders who had finally been forced to choose a side. Ordinary citizens, their only power a desperate courage, stood ready to fight alongside beings whose very existence was the stuff of legend. Nearly two hundred fighters, the last hope of a world on the brink.

"The Great Seal reaches critical activation in six hours," she announced, her voice echoing in the cavernous, roofless chamber. It sounded steadier than she felt. "Our direct assaults have failed. The constructs adapt to every strategy, and the Seal's influence weakens us with every passing minute. We cannot win a conventional fight."

The silence that met her words was heavy with grim acceptance. They all knew it was true. They had thrown themselves against the Citadel's crystalline walls and broken like waves against stone.

"Then we do something unconventional," said a new voice. All eyes turned to Wynne, a Guardian-bonded scholar whose crystal heart had spent decades studying forbidden pre-Sundering texts. She was pale, her academic hands trembling slightly, but her eyes burned with fierce intellect.

"The Council's magic, the Seal itself, is built on a single, fundamental principle: separation," Wynne explained, stepping forward. "It is designed to counter individual bonds, to isolate and destroy. Its power is absolute against singular or even small group targets."

"We've noticed," Dax muttered from the shadows, her voice dripping with sarcasm.

Wynne ignored her. "But the pre-Sundering texts speak of another kind of magic. A cooperative magic, based not on the power of one, but on the harmony of many. They called it a 'choral resonance' or 'soul-weaving'." She took a deep breath. "Theoretically, it would be possible to create a network of interconnected bonds—Guardian and demon spirits

165

working together so closely, their essences so deeply intertwined, that the Seal's magic could not distinguish one from another. It would perceive the network not as two hundred separate targets, but as a single, massive, integrated consciousness."

A murmur of disbelief and wonder ran through the temple.

"You're talking about fusion," Ashfang's voice spoke in Kaela's mind, the thought sharp with alarm. "Temporary merging of spirits *across* bond lines. It's been tried before."

What happened? Kaela asked, her heart sinking.

"Sometimes it worked," he replied. "Sometimes it didn't. When it didn't work... let's just say that separation anxiety becomes a very literal, very fatal problem."

Captain Lyr voiced the same concern. "The level of trust required the precision of timing... We've been allies for weeks, not lifetimes. One mistake, one person falling out of sync, and the backlash could be catastrophic."

"It could tear apart every bond in the network," Wynne confirmed, her voice grim. "We would be linking our souls directly. There is no halfway measure. It is our only hope, but it is a desperate one."

This was it. The precipice. The moment where they chose between a dignified death fighting alone, or a terrifying, uncertain chance at life fighting together. Kaela felt the weight of every gaze, every hope, every fear in the room settle upon her. This was the burden of leadership: not to have all the answers, but to make a choice in the face of uncertainty.

"I won't lie to you," she said, her voice ringing with a conviction that came from some deep well of resolve she didn't know she possessed. "This could kill us all. It is a gamble with our very souls. But the alternative is a certainty. The alternative is watching the Seal complete its work, watching every demon spirit in existence get ripped away from their partners, and knowing we did nothing."

She gestured to the incredible, impossible mixture of beings around her—the Guardian spirits with their noble bearing and radiant power, the demon spirits with their wild intelligence and protective instincts.

"Look around you," she commanded. "Six months ago, half the people in this room would have tried to kill the other half on sight. We were taught to fear each other, to believe we were fundamentally incompatible. And yet here we are. Guardian and demon, light and shadow, working together because we've finally figured out what the Council never understood."

"Which is?" asked Captain Lyr, his voice a low rumble.

"That we're stronger together than apart," Kaela declared, fire beginning to dance around her hands. Ashfang flowed up beside her, his shadows intertwining with her flames in a perfect, familiar harmony. "That cooperation beats domination. That love—real love, the trust between partners who choose each other freely—is the most powerful force in the world. This fusion network won't work if we're doing it out of duty or desperation. It only works if we choose it freely, if we trust each other completely, if we're willing to be vulnerable with people who used to be our enemies."

Captain Lyr was the first to stand, his crystal stag spirit materializing beside him, its light somehow warmer than usual. "I spent my entire career fighting demon-bonded 'criminals.' I was trained to see you as corrupted and dangerous. I was wrong. The corruption was never in you. It was in a system that turned natural diversity into a crime." He looked directly at Kaela. "I don't know if I can link my soul to those I was trained to kill. But I am willing to try. The alternative is a world I cannot bear to live in."

One by one, others followed his lead. Voices rose in the ruined temple, not in a great cheer, but in a series of quiet, personal pledges. A Guardian-bonded rebel offering forgiveness for past persecution. A demon-bonded exile accepting it. An unbonded citizen pledging to support their fight in any way she could. It was a quieter, more profound unity than any battle cry.

"Formation practice," Kaela announced, her heart swelling with a fragile, fierce hope. "We have five hours to learn how to move as one organism. Guardian spirits on the outer ring to face the Seal's light. Demon spirits in the inner circle, providing a core of shadow. Human partners will be the bridge, the living conduits between them."

What followed was the most complex and terrifying magical choreography anyone had ever attempted. The first effort was a disaster. As they tried to link their bonds, a cacophony of spiritual noise erupted—two hundred minds, two hundred spirits, all trying to speak at once. Uncontrolled flares of light and shadow shot across the temple. Several fighters collapsed, clutching their heads as the mental strain became too much.

"Slower!" Kaela called, her own head pounding from the feedback. "We're not racing—we're building something together. Don't impose your rhythm, *feel* for a shared one."

She and Ashfang acted as the anchor. Their bond, forged in exile and tempered in battle, was the most stable in the group. She reached out with her consciousness, not with a command, but with an invitation, a steady rhythm like a heartbeat. *One, two, three, four. In, out. Light, shadow.*

Dax and Mireclaw were the first to sync with them, their poison-and-shadow signature finding a jagged harmony with Kaela's fire-and-shadow. Then Captain Lyr and his stag, their disciplined light softening to match the rhythm. Slowly, painfully, small groups began to find their synchronicity. Triads and quartets of spirits, learning to dance together without stepping on each other's toes.

The practice was grueling. The mental and spiritual exhaustion was immense. To connect your soul so intimately to another was to feel their pain, their fear, their doubt, as keenly as your own. But it was also to feel their courage, their hope, their strength.

With less than two hours to spare, they tried the full formation again.

This time, there was no cacophony. A deep, resonant hum filled the temple as two hundred bonds began to weave together. Kaela felt her consciousness expand, felt Dax's fierce loyalty, Lyr's steady resolve, Wynne's intellectual curiosity, all of it flowing into her, and her own determination flowing back out. For five breathtaking seconds, they were one. One mind, one will, one spirit made of hundreds. The power that blazed between them was terrifying and glorious, a force of creation that could surely shatter the Seal.

Then, a young exile, his bond still new and unstable, lost his focus. A single thread in the tapestry snapped.

The backlash was instant, but contained. Instead of a catastrophic failure, the network simply dissolved, the shared consciousness receding back into individual minds, leaving behind a profound sense of loss and vertigo.

"Again," Kaela said, her voice shaking with effort.

They held it for ten seconds. Then thirty. Then a full minute. It wasn't perfect. It was wildly unstable and incredibly draining. But it was possible.

"Final preparations," Captain Lyr announced, his voice hoarse. "Check your equipment, say your goodbyes. In one hour, we march."

As the fighters dispersed, Kaela stood alone with Ashfang in the temple's heart. Through their bond, she felt his anticipation and fear mirroring her own.

"Any regrets?" she asked, the question feeling impossibly small.

"About bonding with a desperate teenager and ending up here, about to risk total psychic annihilation to save the world?" Ashfang's grin showed his familiar obsidian-dagger teeth. "Not a single one. Whatever happens next, we face it together. As partners."

Kaela nodded, the truth of his words settling into her bones. They were walking into their own destruction, but they were doing it on their own terms, unified by choice. As the coalition began its final, silent march toward the transformed Citadel, Kaela felt a fragile peace settle over her. The Great Seal awaited, a monument to separation and fear. But for the first time, she truly believed they had something stronger. They had each other.

Chapter 20: The Broken Chord

The march on the Citadel was a silent one, a two-hundred-strong procession of ghosts moving through the pre-dawn gloom. There were no battle cries, no rousing speeches. The only sounds were the crunch of boots on the crystalline dust that now coated the city streets and the discordant hum of the Great Seal, a sound that grew from a whisper in the soul to a deafening roar as they approached the transformed fortress. The very air vibrated with its power, a malevolent pressure that sought to pry apart every bond, to remind every spirit of the agony of separation.

Kaela walked at the head of the column, flanked by Dax and Captain Lyr. She could feel the fragile hope of their coalition flickering like a candle in a gale. Each step closer to the Citadel was an act of will, a fight against the spiritual entropy that radiated from Mirren's ritual. Her own bond with Ashfang felt stretched and thin, his presence a comforting warmth she had to actively hold onto against the Seal's relentless pull.

They saw the constructs from a hundred yards out. They weren't patrolling; they were waiting, arranged in a perfect defensive line across the Citadel's main courtyard. They were statues of fused flesh and crystal, mockeries of the Guardian-bonded soldiers they had once been, their eyes glowing with the Seal's hungry white light. There were dozens of them, an army of puppets animated by the will of a single, mad ideal.

"They know we're coming," Captain Lyr stated, his voice a low growl. "Mirren is confident. He's letting us walk right up to his door."

"He's arrogant," Dax countered, her hand resting on the hilt of her blade. "He thinks he's fighting two hundred individuals. He's about to find out he's wrong."

"To your marks!" Kaela's voice cut through the tension. "We form the network on my signal. Hold until the last possible second. We hit them with everything we have at once."

The fighters fanned out, taking the positions they had practiced for hours in the ruined temple. Guardian-bonded rebels formed the outer ring, their spirits blazing like miniature suns, ready to meet the Seal's light head-on. The demon-bonded exiles gathered in the center, a core of living shadow prepared to anchor their assault. And between them stood the humans—the rebels, the exiles, the citizens—the living bridges who would weave the disparate threads into a single, unbreakable cord.

Kaela took her place at the very heart of the formation. She closed her eyes, shutting out the sight of the approaching constructs, and reached inward. *Ashfang?*

Always, his voice came back, a pillar of strength in the swirling chaos of her mind. *Let's show them what real unity looks like.*

"Now!" she screamed, throwing her consciousness outward not as a command, but as an invitation.

The fusion network ignited.

For a single, breathtaking moment, it was more glorious than anything they had achieved in practice. The oppressive hum of the Seal was replaced by a resonant, choral harmony as two hundred bonds, four hundred spirits, locked into perfect synchronicity. Kaela felt her mind explode outward, her consciousness merging with every other fighter in the coalition. She felt Dax's fierce, protective loyalty, Captain Lyr's unbending resolve, Wynne's brilliant, analytical mind, the quiet courage of the citizen-fighters, the ancient wisdom of spirits who had not touched each other in five hundred years. They were a galaxy of souls united, a single being of unimaginable power and purpose. The constructs were no longer just targets; she could feel the faint, trapped echoes of the people they used to be, and she would set them free.

"**STRIKE!**"

The voice was not hers alone; it was the voice of the collective, and it commanded with the force of creation. A wave of perfectly harmonized energy—light and shadow, order and chaos, life and death, all woven together—erupted from the formation. It struck the first line of constructs not as a physical blow, but as a spiritual solvent. The crystalline forms cracked, dissolved, and evaporated, releasing the tormented spirits within, which vanished with cries of gratitude.

It was working. The constructs, designed to fight individuals, had no defense against a unified consciousness. They shattered a dozen of them in the first volley. A cheer, mental and vocal, rippled through the network. They surged forward, ready to deliver the final blow that would break the Citadel's defenses and carry them to Mirren's chamber.

And that was when the Great Seal fought back.

It wasn't a counter-attack. It was something far more insidious. A wave of pure conceptual force washed over them, a spiritual poison aimed not at their bodies, but at the very connections that held them together. It was the essence of separation, of discord. Every buried doubt, every lingering prejudice, every flicker of fear was seized, amplified, and turned into a weapon.

A Guardian-bonded traditionalist, linked to a demon of shadow, suddenly felt a spike of five hundred years of ingrained terror—*corruption, filth, abomination.*

A demon spirit, intertwined with a Guardian of pure light, felt an instinctive recoil from the searing purity—*pain, judgment, annihilation.*

The young exile from their practice session felt his insecurity flare into outright panic—*I'm not strong enough, I'm going to fail, I'm going to kill us all!*

Kaela felt it all, a thousand points of friction tearing at the perfect harmony of their network. She fought to hold it together, pouring her own strength and

Ashfang's into the fraying connections, trying to soothe the rising panic. *Trust each other! We are stronger together! Don't let him divide us!*

But the Seal was relentless. It was a weapon built by a master of division, and it knew every weakness in the mortal soul. The harmony faltered, becoming a jagged, painful dissonance. The single, unified chord of their consciousness began to fray into hundreds of screaming, individual notes.

The young exile's nerve broke.

His panicked thought—*I can't do this!*—was the final snap in the overwrought tapestry. His bond buckled, and the network didn't just dissolve. It imploded.

The backlash hit Kaela like a star exploding in her skull. As the anchor, she was the focal point for the combined spiritual agony of two hundred shattered connections. The power they had raised didn't just vanish; it recoiled inward along the pathways they had built, tearing through them with devastating force.

She felt her very soul being shredded. The delicate, intricate lacework of her bond with Ashfang, the connection that had been the center of her existence for months, was ripped apart with an agony that transcended physical pain. It was the pain of amputation, of being torn from a part of herself she hadn't known was missing until she'd found it.

Her scream was not human. It was the sound of a spirit dying, of a bond being broken, of a hope being utterly and finally extinguished. The sound itself threw fighters to the ground, their own bonds reeling in sympathetic torment.

Then, darkness. A welcome, silent, empty void.

When she woke, the world had changed.

She was lying on the cold ground in the ruins of the temple, their makeshift command center now a triage station for the wounded. The first thing she noticed was not the pain in her head or the concerned face of Dax leaning over her. It was the silence.

The profound, deafening, soul-crushing silence in her own mind was a physical presence. It felt like a phantom limb, a gaping wound where half her soul used to be. Every breath was a conscious effort, her own heartbeat a lonely, alien drum in the crushing emptiness. This was the cost of failure: not just defeat, but a hollowing out of her very being.

The constant hum of Ashfang's presence, the sarcastic commentary, the steady warmth, the shared consciousness that had been her anchor since Naming Day—it was gone. She reached for it, desperately, with a part of her that was more instinct than thought, and found nothing. Just a void. An empty space where half of her soul used to be.

"Ashfang?" The name was a ragged whisper.

"He's... here," Dax said, her voice strained. She helped Kaela sit up.

Kaela's frantic gaze swept the room until she saw him. He was a flicker. A smudge of darkness in the corner, barely more substantial than a shadow, wavering in and out of existence. His ember eyes, usually so bright with intelligence and wit, were dull and distant. The bond between them wasn't gone entirely, she realized, but it was severed. A frayed, useless thread where a steel cable had once been.

"What happened?" Kaela asked, the words tasting like ash. "How long...?"

"Two hours," Captain Lyr replied, his face a grim mask of defeat. He was helping Wynne tend to a fighter whose spirit was flickering as badly as Ashfang's. "The network collapse was... catastrophic. You bore the brunt of it. When you fell, the constructs advanced. We were being slaughtered. We had to retreat."

Her eyes took in the scene. Seven bodies lay under canvas sheets. Dozens of fighters were wounded, their bonds damaged, their spirits weak. The confident army that had marched on the Citadel was a broken, huddled mass of survivors.

The fusion network, their desperate, beautiful hope, had not just failed. It had been their ruin. And as Kaela stared at the empty space in her soul where her partner used to be, she understood that the Great Seal had already won. It had taken everything that mattered.

A profound and hopeless silence settled over the ruined temple, broken only by the quiet sobs of the wounded and the distant, triumphant hum of the Seal. It was over. They had lost.

Chapter 21: The Weight of Ash

The first thing Kaela knew was the silence.

It was not the absence of sound—she could hear the quiet groans of the wounded, the distant crackle of a fire, the whisper of voices from across the ruined temple. It was the silence inside her own skull, a profound and terrifying emptiness where the constant, comforting hum of Ashfang's presence had been for months. The void felt like a physical wound, a phantom limb that ached with an agony deeper than any broken bone.

She pushed herself into a sitting position, and the world tilted violently. Vertigo slammed into her, a nauseating disorientation that came from losing a sixth sense she hadn't known she possessed until it was gone. For months, Ashfang's presence had been her compass, a constant point of reference in the spiritual chaos of the world. Without him, her own body felt alien, a vessel adrift on a vast, empty sea. The world seemed too sharp, the colors oversaturated and painful, her own heartbeat a lonely, alien drum in the crushing quiet.

She reached for the bond, the instinct as natural as breathing, and found only frayed threads leading to a hollow space.

179

Ashfang? The thought was a raw, silent scream into the void.

There was a flicker of response, not a voice or a feeling, but a distant echo of shared pain, like seeing a familiar face through a mile of murky water. Her gaze swept the temple, frantic, until she saw him. He was a smudge of darkness in the corner, a wavering heat-haze of shadow, barely more substantial than smoke. His ember eyes, usually so bright with wit and intelligence, were dull and distant.

Stumbling, she made her way to him, each step a monumental effort. As she drew closer, she could feel the coldness of the space between them, a dead zone where the warmth of their connection used to be. They were severed. Not completely gone, but cut off, two islands of consciousness where once there had been a continent.

"Ashfang," she whispered, her voice cracking. She reached out a hand, stopping just short of his flickering form. "Can you... can you hear me?"

His form solidified for a bare second, a shudder of effort passing through him. The ember eyes focused on her, and for an instant, she felt a ghost of their bond—a wave of agony, terror, and a fierce, desperate protectiveness that was so quintessentially *him*. Then it was gone, and he dissolved back into a barely coherent shadow. He was fighting just to exist.

Panic, cold and sharp, clawed at her throat. She needed to feel the fire, to know that part of her was still there. She held out a trembling hand, concentrating, calling on the power that had become her identity.

A flame sputtered to life in her palm. It was a pathetic thing, the size of a candle flame, flickering and pale. It gave off no heat. It felt... foreign. A tool she was holding, not a part of herself. The effort of summoning even this small spark left her feeling hollowed out, a bone-deep chill spreading through her limbs. This was the cost of failure. Not just defeat, but the loss of herself.

"Don't," a voice rasped.

Kaela looked up to see Dax kneeling beside her, her face smudged with soot and streaked with tears she had clearly tried to wipe away. Mireclaw was coiled loosely on her shoulders, its usually vibrant scales now a dull, sickly green. There was a crude bandage on Dax's shoulder, stained with dark blood.

"Don't do that to yourself," Dax repeated, her voice brittle. "You need to rest. What's left of you, anyway."

The unspoken accusation hung in the air between them: *this is your fault.*

"Dax, I..." Kaela's voice broke. "I'm so sorry."

"Sorry?" Dax let out a short, bitter laugh that was closer to a sob. "Tell that to Elara. And Joric. And Rhys. Sorry won't bring Ember back. It won't un-break the bonds your plan shattered. It won't stop the Seal from finishing its work in... what is it, Wynne? Four hours?"

181

"Three and a half," came the scholar's tired voice from across the temple.

Kaela flinched, the names of the dead landing like physical blows. The weight of it all—the faces of the fallen, the wounded, the ticking clock, the deafening silence in her own soul—was crushing. "You're right," she whispered. "It was my mistake. I pushed too hard. I thought..."

"You thought you could save everyone," Dax finished, the anger in her voice finally dissolving into pure, gut-wrenching grief. "She did, too. That was Ember's problem. Always trying to fix everything."

Tears began to stream down Dax's face. "She wasn't just our healer, Kaela. Do you remember that time she tried to teach Mireclaw to fetch? She spent a solid week, every morning, trying to convince a venomous serpent that a thrown stick was an interesting and worthwhile toy. She brought him a different stick each day—birch, oak, willow. She said she thought he might have a preference."

A wet, choked laugh escaped Kaela's lips at the memory. She remembered Ember's patient frustration, the way Mireclaw would just stare at the stick and then at Ember as if she'd lost her mind. It was a memory of a time that felt a lifetime ago, a time of peace and simple absurdities.

"She never gave up," Kaela said softly.

"No," Dax whispered, wiping her eyes with the back of her hand. "She never did. Not on a stubborn serpent, and not on a collapsing fusion network." She looked at Kaela, her eyes red-rimmed but clear.

182

"She believed in you. In what you were trying to build. We all did."

"And I led you into a slaughter," Kaela said, the guilt a physical weight in her chest.

"You led us into a fight we chose," Dax corrected, her voice regaining a sliver of its old strength. "Don't you dare take that away from us. Don't you dare take it away from her."

Dax stood up, her movements stiff with pain. "So what now, leader? We sit here and wait for the end? We let Mirren win? We let Ember's sacrifice be for nothing?" The question was meant to be a challenge, but all Kaela felt was the vast, empty truth. They had lost. Their best weapon had been turned against them. Their army was broken. She was broken. Hope was a luxury they could no longer afford.

"Maybe there's nothing left to do," Kaela murmured, looking at her hands, which felt like a stranger's. "Maybe... maybe the Council was right. Maybe we are too dangerous. Maybe this is what happens when you fight against the natural order." Dax stared at her for a long moment, then shook her head in disgust and walked away, leaving Kaela alone with her despair.

She sat there for what felt like an eternity, adrift in the silence of her own mind. She watched the wounded being tended to. She saw Wynne, the scholar, staring blankly at a pre-Sundering text, her brilliant mind finally beaten. She saw two partners, a Guardian-bonded rebel and a demon-bonded exile, huddled together, their spirits flickering weakly as they tried to draw comfort from each other's presence. This was her army now: a collection of ghosts haunted by their own hope.

These were the people who had followed her. The ones who had chosen to hope when everything told them to despair. Ember had died for that hope. The young exile whose panic had shattered the network had died for it. They had all been willing to risk everything for a chance at something better.

Her gaze drifted back to Ashfang's flickering form. He was still there. Wounded, distant, but not gone. He hadn't given up, even with their bond in tatters. He was fighting to simply exist.

The despair in her chest didn't vanish. The grief didn't lessen. But something new began to form in the cold, quiet space where her hope used to be. It was not the fiery confidence of a righteous crusader. It was the cold, hard resolve of someone who had already lost everything that mattered. A grim, quiet determination.

Ember's sacrifice will not be for nothing. Their deaths will not be for nothing.

The thought was not a shout; it was a whisper in the silent cathedral of her soul. It was a promise.

Slowly, painfully, Kaela pushed herself to her feet. She ignored the vertigo, the ache of her broken bond, the crushing weight of her failure. She walked across the temple, her steps unsteady but purposeful, toward the small group huddled around the stolen Citadel maps. Captain Lyr looked up as she approached, his expression weary but questioning.

Kaela looked at the map, at the fortress that had broken them. The silence in her head was no longer an emptiness. It was a quiet space where a single, cold thought had taken root.

"There's another way," she said. The words, spoken so quietly, cut through the temple's despair like a shard of glass. Every head turned toward Kaela.

Captain Lyr looked up from the Citadel map, his expression a mixture of grief and disbelief. "Another way? Kaela, we've lost half our fighters. Our spirits are weakened. Their defenses have adapted to everything we've thrown at them."

"We've been trying to meet Mirren on his terms," Kaela said, her voice still quiet but now infused with a cold, hard certainty. "With overwhelming power. We've been playing his game." She stepped toward the altar, her finger tracing a line on a different document—the scrolls of intelligence they had seized after Kade Thistle's betrayal. "But Kade gave us something more valuable than troop movements. He gave us Mirren's own arrogance."

She pointed to a specific diagram on the scroll, a detail they had all overlooked in their focus on a frontal assault. "This is a service schematic for the Citadel, pre-Sundering. Kade confirmed it's still accurate. Mirren's entire defense is focused outward—on the courtyard, the main gates, the sky. He's expecting another army. He is not expecting a scalpel."

Hope, fragile and painful, began to dawn on the faces around the map. Lyr leaned in closer, tracing a thin, forgotten line. "An old aqueduct," he breathed.

"Sealed for centuries, but Kade's contact mentioned it was never filled. It runs directly beneath the old foundation..."

"...and emerges into a ventilation shaft just below the primary ritual chamber," Kaela finished for him.

"He wouldn't leave it unguarded," Dax argued, though the fight was returning to her eyes.

"Why wouldn't he?" Lyr countered. "It's a forgotten relic. And all his constructs, all his power, is engaged in holding the perimeter. He's left the heart of his fortress vulnerable because he believes we have no way to reach it."

A new energy filled the room—not the fiery hope of their previous attempt, but the grim determination of survivors with one last, desperate card to play. This was not a plan for a glorious victory. This was a plan for a final, desperate act of defiance.

"It's a suicide mission," Dax said, but she was already checking the edge on her blade. "A small team, moving fast." "And quiet," Kaela added. The silence in her head remained, a gaping wound, but this final chance was a sliver of light in the darkness. "We can't fight the constructs. We have to move past them, unheard and unseen."

She pushed herself fully upright, ignoring the wave of vertigo that came with the movement. She looked at the faces around her—broken, exhausted, but not yet defeated. "I won't order anyone to do this," she said, her voice clear and steady. "The fusion network was my mistake, and I won't ask anyone else to pay for it. But I'm going. We have less than four hours to stop that ritual." She took a deep breath. "I need a small team. Twenty volunteers. We go in quiet, we disrupt the ritual, and we either succeed or we don't come back. Who's with me?"

For a moment, only the sound of the crackling fire filled the temple. Then Dax stepped forward, her movement stiff but her gaze unwavering. Captain Lyr was next, giving a single, decisive nod. One by one, others joined them—Guardian-bonded rebels whose spirits pulsed with grim light, demon-bonded exiles whose shadows clung to them like cloaks of resolve, and even a handful of the unbonded citizens who had proven their courage in the street war.

There were no rousing speeches, no boasts of victory. It was a silent, solemn pledge made by those who had already lost too much to turn back now. Within a minute, twenty volunteers stood with her. Kaela felt a faint flicker from Ashfang's distant consciousness—not of strength, but of presence. He was with her.

They all were. The final assault would not be a desperate charge; it would be a quiet promise kept in the heart of the storm.

Chapter 22: Shatter the Seal

The path Kade's intelligence had revealed was a ghost passage, an artery of the old Citadel forgotten by its modern masters. With the fortress's main forces and all of Mirren's attention focused on the brutal battle raging at the perimeter, the Citadel's heart was left unguarded. They moved like whispers through its forgotten veins, the screams and explosions from the courtyard providing the perfect cover for their silent infiltration.

The ritual chamber at the heart of the transformed Citadel was a cathedral of crystalline horror.

Kaela and her twenty volunteers pressed themselves against the chamber's entrance, staring in awe and terror at what Mirren had created. The room stretched impossibly high, its walls covered in living crystal that pulsed with that hungry white light. At the center, suspended in a web of silver energy, was the Great Seal itself—not a physical object, but a rent in reality that showed the void between worlds.

And around it, chanting in perfect unison, stood the remains of the Council of Light.

"They're not human anymore," whispered Captain Lyr, his crystal stag spirit trembling beside him.

He was right. The Councilors had been transformed by their proximity to the Seal, their forms becoming hybrid creatures of flesh and crystal. They moved with mechanical precision, their voices carrying harmonics that belonged to no living throat.

"The ritual's almost complete," the Guardian-bonded scholar observed, studying the energy patterns that swirled around the chamber. "Maybe five minutes before the Seal reaches critical activation."

"Then we move now," Kaela said, though her damaged bond with Ashfang made it hard to feel confident about anything. His presence was barely a whisper in her mind, more memory than reality.

"Wait." Dax grabbed her arm as she started to move forward. "Look at the center. Look at what he's doing."

Kaela followed her gaze and felt her blood turn to ice. Suspended above the Great Seal, held in place by crackling energy fields, were dozens of demon spirits—not bonded to anyone, but trapped, helpless, slowly being torn apart to fuel the ritual. She recognized some of them from the early days of the resistance, demons whose partners had been killed or severed but who had somehow survived on their own.

And there, barely visible in the writhing mass of shadow and pain, was a familiar horned silhouette.

"Ashfang," she breathed.

Somehow, some part of him had been pulled into the Seal's influence. Not his full essence—she could still feel their weakened bond—but enough to cause him agony and strengthen Mirren's ritual.

"It's a trap within a trap," Captain Lyr said grimly. "He's using our demons against us, making sure we can't attack without risking their destruction."

"Then we don't attack," Kaela said, surprising everyone including herself. "We do something else."

"Such as?"

"We give them what they've never had before." Kaela stepped into the chamber, her hands empty of weapons, her voice carrying clearly across the crystalline space. "Freedom to choose."

The chanting faltered as the transformed Councilors noticed their intrusion. Mirren himself turned from the Seal, his dual nature now fully visible—light and shadow writhing around him in patterns that hurt to look at directly.

"Kaela Veyne," he said, his voice carrying the harmonics of both his spirits. "How good of you to witness the completion of my work. In moments, every demon spirit in existence will be severed permanently, and humanity will finally know peace."

"Whose peace?" Kaela asked, walking slowly toward the center of the chamber while her volunteers spread out behind her. "Yours? The Council's? Or the peace of the grave?"

"The peace of order. The peace of knowing that chaos can never again threaten civilization."

"Chaos." Kaela gestured to the trapped demons above them, their forms writhing in agony. "Is that what you call the desire to exist freely? To choose your own bonds, your own purpose?"

Mirren let out a short, pitying laugh. "You call this chaos freedom? I have seen what true Eidolons do with their power, child. I have read the forbidden histories. I saw them level cities for a whim, treat humans as disposable playthings. The Sundering wasn't a crime—it was a necessity! A terrible, painful culling that brought five centuries of peace! A peace you are throwing away for a sentimental fantasy."

"I call it the fundamental flaw in creation—the mistake that the original Sundering was meant to correct." Mirren raised his hands, and the Great Seal pulsed with increasing intensity. "But I won't make my predecessors' error. I won't leave the work half-finished."

"No," Kaela agreed. "You won't."

She reached out through her damaged bond, not to Ashfang—their connection was too weak—but to something else. To the network of relationships she'd built over months of desperate cooperation. To the trust that had grown between former enemies. To the love that had flourished in the spaces between light and shadow.

"Now," she called.

Twenty volunteers stepped forward in perfect unison, their spirits blazing with coordinated light. But instead of attacking the Seal or its defenders, they did something unprecedented.

They offered themselves to the trapped demons.

Not permanent bonds—there wasn't time for that level of commitment. But temporary partnerships, freely given, no coercion or desperation involved. Just the simple offer: join us, work with us, be part of something larger than yourself.

The initial response was a wave of raw, terrified hope from the trapped demons. But Mirren's ritual fought back. The Great Seal, a weapon of pure division, lashed out not with force, but with poison. It amplified the five hundred years of ingrained fear and prejudice between the two types of spirits.

Kaela felt it as a wave of psychic dissonance. The Guardian spirits of her volunteers recoiled, their pure light instinctively flinching from the chaotic, wounded darkness of the demons. The demon spirits, in turn, felt the Guardians' light not as an offer of help, but as the searing judgment of their ancient captors. The nascent connections sputtered, threatening to break.

"No," Mirren hissed, a triumphant sneer twisting his features. "You see? Separation is the natural order! Even when offered a choice, they reject each other!"

He was wrong. Kaela knew he was wrong, but the Seal was using their own history against them. Force wouldn't work. Pushing them together would only increase the friction.

Then, from the silent, wounded space where her bond with Ashfang used to be, a memory surfaced— Ember's patient voice in the Shadebond camp. *Feel, name, channel, balance.* It wasn't just a training technique. It was the answer. It was the only answer.

She projected the thought to the twenty volunteers, not as a command, but as a shared lesson, a desperate plea.

Feel it, she sent, her thought echoing in the minds of her allies. *Don't* fight the fear. The *Seal is showing you five centuries of lies. Feel the revulsion, the prejudice, the pain of being torn apart.*

She felt the volunteers flinch, but they held their ground, their trust in her overriding their instinct to pull back.

Now, name it, Kaela continued, her own consciousness embracing the agony. *It is not your fear. It is a weapon. It is the echo of a crime. Name it 'the lie.'*

A subtle shift occurred in the chamber's spiritual atmosphere. The fear, once acknowledged and labeled, lost its overwhelming power. It was no longer a visceral reaction, but an external force to be examined.

Channel it, she urged, her voice in their minds growing stronger. *Take* that energy—all that pain and fear—and transform it. *Channel it into a shared desire. Not a desire to fight, but a desire to be whole. A desire for this agony of separation to finally end.*

The chaotic energy in the room began to coalesce. The raw fear became a focused, unified yearning. The final piece was the hardest.

Balance, Kaela commanded, and this was for the spirits themselves. She focused on Captain Lyr's stag and the shadow-deer it was hesitating to approach. **Offer** your balance. Guardian, offer your stability to the demon's chaos. Demon, offer your adaptability to the Guardian's rigidity. You are not master and slave. You **are not pure and corrupt. You are two halves of a single, beautiful whole. Find your balance.**

That's when it happened.

It was not a sudden, magical cataclysm. It was a choice. A hundred quiet, individual moments of courage. A Guardian phoenix consciously softening its light to welcome a raven of shadow. A serpent of pure light deliberately weaving itself through Dax's Mireclaw, trusting that its poison would not harm it. And across the chamber, every spirit, guided by the mantra, made the choice to trust its other half.

The crystal stag spirit beside Captain Lyr flowed together with a shadow-deer that had materialized from the freed demons. A Guardian phoenix merged with a demon raven in a explosion of fire and starlight. Dax's Mireclaw intertwined with a serpent of pure light, becoming something that was both poison and medicine, death and healing.

And Ashfang...

Kaela felt him return to her consciousness with such force that she gasped aloud. But he wasn't alone. Flowing with him was a sky serpent of brilliant gold—Aurelia, whose Guardian half had been bonded to one of the volunteers but whose demon aspect had been trapped in the Seal's web.

Together, they became Ignivane—a being of perfect balance, flame and wind united in a form that blazed with creative destruction.

"This is what we really are," Kaela said, her voice now carrying the harmonics of three separate beings working as one. "Not light or shadow, not Guardian or demon, but whole. Complete. Free to choose our own nature instead of having it chosen for us."

Around the chamber, other Eidolons were forming—spirits reuniting with halves they'd been separated from for centuries, becoming what they'd always been meant to be. The Great Seal, designed to maintain eternal separation, began to crack under the pressure of so much unified consciousness.

"No!" Mirren's scream was inhuman, desperate. "I won't let you undo centuries of progress! I won't let chaos return!"

He threw himself into the Seal's energy, trying to force it back to stability through sheer will. For a moment, it looked like he might succeed—the crystal walls reinforced themselves, the separation energy intensified.

But then Kaela understood what needed to happen.

"We don't destroy the Seal," she called to the assembled Eidolons. "We complete it."

Instead of fighting against the Great Seal's power, they embraced it. Used it. Turned it from a weapon of separation into a tool of unity. The ritual that had been designed to tear apart bonds became the mechanism for creating new ones—not just between individual spirits and humans, but between all the fragments of creation that had been artificially divided.

The change rippled outward from the chamber like a wave, spreading across Calyss, across the continent, across the world. Everywhere the Great Seal's influence had reached, the barriers between light and shadow began to dissolve.

Mirren's final scream was cut short as his own forced dual bond finally found balance—not the domination of one aspect over another, but true partnership. His unicorn and his corrupted seraph flowed together, becoming an Eidolon of judgment tempered by mercy.

The transformation destroyed him as an individual— the man who had spent centuries trying to control the nature of existence simply couldn't survive the revelation that control had never been the point.

As the Great Seal completed its work and then dissolved, leaving behind not separation but connection, Kaela felt Ignivane's consciousness settling into something stable. Three beings choosing to be one, not through compulsion or desperation, but through love.

"Is it over?" Captain Lyr asked, his voice now carrying the harmonics of the wolf-stag Eidolon he'd become.

"The ritual's over," Kaela replied, looking around at the chamber full of unified beings. "But what comes next... that's up to all of us."

Through the crystalline walls, she could see the dawn breaking over Calyss—the first sunrise in five centuries to shine on a world where spirits were free to be whole.

They'd done it. Not through overwhelming force or individual heroics, but through the simple act of choosing cooperation over domination, unity over separation, love over fear.

The age of the Sundering was finally over. The age of wholeness was about to begin.

Chapter 23: Aftermath in Ash

The city of Calyss woke to a world that no longer made sense.

Kaela stood on the balcony of what had once been the Council chamber, looking out over streets where five centuries of certainty had crumbled overnight. The crystalline growths that had consumed the Citadel were dissolving like salt in rain, leaving behind buildings that seemed somehow more solid, more real than they had before the transformation.

But it was the people that drew her attention.

In the square below, she could see them gathering— former enemies standing side by side, trying to understand what had happened to their world. Guardian-bonded citizens whose spirits were suddenly flickering between light and shadow. Ordinary people who had never been bonded at all but were now sensing spiritual presences they couldn't quite identify. And scattered throughout the crowd, the Eidolons—beings of unified consciousness who moved with an otherworldly grace that made everyone around them stop and stare.

"Overwhelming, isn't it?" said a familiar voice behind her.

Kaela turned to see Captain Lyr approaching, though he was no longer exactly the man she'd known. The wolf-stag Eidolon he'd become was still recognizably him, but there was something deeper there now—a wholeness that radiated calm authority.

"I keep expecting someone to tell us what to do next," she admitted. "The Council's gone, the old laws don't apply anymore, and half the population doesn't understand what's happened to them."

"Do you?"

Kaela considered the question while she reached out through her connection to Ignivane. The triple consciousness felt natural now—not the overwhelming rush of the first fusion, but something as comfortable as breathing. Ashfang's sardonic wit, Aurelia's fierce intelligence, and her own stubborn determination had woven together into something larger than any of them alone.

"I understand that we broke something that was holding the world apart," she said finally. "Whether what we've built to replace it will actually work... that's still an open question."

"The emergency council is convening in an hour," Captain Lyr informed her. "Representatives from every faction that survived the transformation. Guardian-bonded, demon-bonded, Eidolons, ordinary citizens, even some of the former Council loyalists who want to negotiate rather than fight."

"Negotiate what?"

"How to govern a city where the old rules don't apply anymore. How to handle people whose spirits are still unstable from the transformation. How to deal with the fact that about half our population has suddenly gained access to magical abilities they don't understand."

Kaela rubbed her temples, feeling a headache building. Destroying the old system had been the easy part, relatively speaking. Building something better to replace it was going to be infinitely more complex.

"Any word from the outer districts?" she asked.

"Mixed reports. Some towns are celebrating— apparently they've been quietly harboring demon-bonded refugees for years and are relieved they don't have to hide anymore. Others are... less enthusiastic about the changes."

"And the Borderlands?"

"Complete chaos, but the productive kind. Farmers whose Guardian spirits have suddenly gained demon aspects are discovering they can accelerate crop growth and control pests simultaneously. Merchants are reporting that trade routes that have been dangerous for centuries are suddenly safe because the 'wild' spirits are no longer hostile."

That was something, at least. The transformation hadn't just affected human settlements—it had rippled through the entire magical ecosystem, healing divisions that had existed since the original Sundering.

"Casualties?" Kaela asked, though she dreaded the answer.

"Lower than expected, surprisingly. The transformation was traumatic for everyone, but most people seem to be adapting." Captain Lyr's expression grew troubled. "Though we've lost about a dozen to spiritual shock—people whose bonds were too damaged to handle the sudden change."

Each death felt like a personal failure, even though Kaela knew intellectually that the alternative would have been the extinction of every demon spirit in existence. But knowing something and feeling it were different challenges entirely.

"Dax wants to see you," Captain Lyr continued. "She's setting up triage stations for people whose transformations are still unstable."

Kaela found her friend in the ruins of the old Guardian hospital, which had been hastily converted into a treatment center for transformation-related injuries. The building hummed with organized chaos—healers working alongside Eidolons whose unified consciousness made them naturally gifted at spiritual repair, families bringing relatives whose bonds had been disrupted by the change, and a steady stream of ordinary citizens seeking reassurance that they weren't going insane.

"Status report," Kaela said, approaching the makeshift command center where Dax was coordinating relief efforts.

"Could be worse," Dax replied, her own transformation having created an interesting partnership between Mireclaw and a Guardian serpent of pure healing light. The combination made her uniquely qualified to help people whose light and shadow aspects were struggling to integrate. "Most of the severe cases are people who already had damaged bonds from Council 'treatments.' The transformation is trying to heal them, but some wounds run too deep."

"Can we help them?"

"Some of them. The ones whose spirits are willing to try integration again. But others..." She gestured toward a section of the hospital where people sat quietly, their eyes empty of the spiritual light that now seemed universal. "Some bonds were too broken to repair. They're not quite Hollow, but they're not whole either."

Kaela felt a pang of guilt. In all their planning for the transformation, they'd focused on the people it would help, not the ones it might hurt.

"There's something else," Dax continued. "We're getting reports of new bonds forming spontaneously. Children who were too young for Naming Day ceremonies suddenly manifesting spirit connections. Adults who were Hollow their entire lives waking up with Eidolon consciousness."

"Is that... normal?"

"Nothing about this is normal. But it seems stable so far." Dax's expression grew thoughtful. "It's like the transformation didn't just heal existing bonds—it opened up possibilities that never existed before."

They were interrupted by a commotion from the hospital's main entrance. A group of former Council enforcers was trying to bring in their wounded captain, but the man was fighting them every step of the way.

"I don't need treatment from demon-lovers," he was shouting, his Guardian eagle spirit fluttering weakly around his shoulders. "I'd rather die than accept corruption!"

"Sir," one of his subordinates pleaded, "your spirit is dying. The transformation tried to integrate it with a shadow aspect, but your resistance is tearing the bond apart."

Kaela approached carefully, recognizing the captain as someone who'd been present during some of the early confrontations. He'd been a true believer in the Council's ideology, completely convinced that demon spirits were inherently evil.

"Captain," she said gently, "your eagle wants to live. But it can't survive in a world where integration is the natural state. You're fighting your own spiritual healing."

"Because healing means accepting corruption," he spat. "I won't betray everything I've believed my entire life."

"What if everything you believed was wrong?"

The question hung in the air between them. Around the hospital, conversations quieted as people waited to see how this confrontation would resolve.

"The Council taught you that purity was strength," Kaela continued. "That separation was safety. But look around you. Look at what cooperation has accomplished that domination never could."

She gestured to the healing work happening throughout the hospital—former enemies working together, light and shadow spirits collaborating to repair damages that neither could have fixed alone.

"Your eagle doesn't want to be pure," she said. "It wants to be whole. The choice is whether you're going to help it or keep fighting it until you both die."

For a long moment, the captain stared at her with the kind of hatred that came from having your worldview challenged. Then his gaze shifted to his eagle spirit, whose light was growing dimmer by the minute. "If I let this happen," he said quietly, "I won't be the same person anymore." "No," Kaela agreed. "You'll be more than you were before."

The transformation, when it finally happened, was gentle—nothing like the explosive fusion she'd experienced. The captain's eagle spirit simply... expanded, revealing shadow aspects that had always been there but had been suppressed by years of conditioning. The man himself seemed to grow lighter, as if a weight he'd been carrying for decades had finally been lifted.

"I can feel it," he whispered, staring at his hands where light and shadow danced together. "The connection I've been missing my whole life." "That's what we've all been missing," Kaela said. "The Council convinced us that we were supposed to be half-people, that wholeness was impossible. But it was always there, waiting for us to stop fighting it."

As the day wore on, similar scenes played out throughout the city. People who had spent their lives believing in separation slowly learning to embrace integration. Children who had been afraid of their own shadows discovering that darkness wasn't evil, just different. Adults who had thought themselves broken realizing they were simply incomplete.

Not everyone adapted easily. Some former Council loyalists chose exile rather than acceptance of the new reality. Some demon-bonded people struggled with the sudden responsibility of being examples rather than outcasts. And some ordinary citizens found the rapid change too overwhelming to handle.

But for every person who couldn't adapt, there were ten who embraced the transformation with joy and relief. The city that had been built on rigid hierarchy was slowly reorganizing itself around principles of cooperation and mutual support.

"It's going to work," Dax said as they watched the sunset from the hospital's roof, the day's crisis finally under control. "Not perfectly, not without problems, but... it's going to work."

"The hard part's just beginning," Kaela replied, though she found herself smiling. "We have to build new institutions, new laws, new ways of handling conflicts between people whose capabilities we're still figuring out."

"But we don't have to do it alone," Dax pointed out. "That's the difference between us and the Council. They tried to control everything from the top down.

We're building from the bottom up, with input from everyone who's affected."

Through her connection to Ignivane, Kaela could feel the truth of those words. Across the city, people were organizing themselves into voluntary associations, working groups, mutual aid societies. Not because they were told to, but because cooperation felt natural when you weren't constantly fighting half of yourself.

"Ember would have loved this," she said quietly.
"She did love this," Dax corrected. "She died making it possible."

As the first stars appeared in the darkening sky, Kaela felt...peace. Not the absence of conflict—there would always be challenges, disagreements, problems to solve. But the peace of knowing that those challenges would be met by people working together instead of being torn apart by artificial divisions.

The age of the Sundering was over. The age of wholeness had begun. And despite everything it had cost them, despite all the pain and loss and uncertainty that lay ahead, Kaela found herself looking forward to finding out what they could build together.

Chapter 24: The Reckonings

The letter arrived three days after the transformation, delivered by a nervous courier who looked like he'd rather be anywhere else in the world.

Kaela recognized her mother's handwriting immediately—the same careful script that had labeled her childhood belongings, written shopping lists, and penned the note she'd treasured during her early days of exile. But now those familiar loops and curves carried a weight of uncertainty that made her hands shake as she broke the seal.

Dearest Kaela,

We don't know if you're alive. We don't know if you'll receive this. We don't even know if the daughter who reads these words is still the same person who was exiled from our home four months ago.

But we need to see you. Not to demand explanations or assign blame, but to understand what our world has become—and what role we played in almost destroying it.

Your father's shop has been transformed. The Guardian-blessed tools he's worked with for thirty years now carry shadows as well as light, and they're more efficient than they've ever been. The neighbors who once whispered about having a "corrupted" daughter now ask if we know how to contact you, because their own children are manifesting Eidolon consciousness and they don't understand what's happening.

We were wrong, Kaela. About everything. The Council told us that loving you meant helping you become "pure," but what we should have done was love you enough to let you be whole.

Please come home. Not as the girl we tried to fix, but as the woman you chose to become.

With all our love and regret, Mother and Father

Kaela read the letter three times before she could trust her voice enough to speak. Through her connection to Ignivane, she felt Ashfang's gentle amusement and Aurelia's protective concern, but also something else—a deep wellspring of compassion that belonged to all three of them together.

"Good news or complicated news?" Dax asked, looking up from the reports she'd been reviewing. The provisional government they'd established was drowning in paperwork as people tried to figure out how to live in a world where the old rules no longer applied.

"Both," Kaela replied, folding the letter carefully. "My parents want to see me."

"About time. You've been avoiding that conversation for weeks."

It was true. In the chaos of establishing new institutions and helping people adapt to their transformations, Kaela had found a dozen reasons not to return to the house where she'd grown up. Part of it was logistics—she was needed here, in the city, where the largest concentration of problems required attention. But mostly it was fear.

Fear that her parents would reject the person she'd become. Fear that they'd try to hold onto the memory of who she'd been before her exile. Fear that the love they offered would come with conditions she could no longer meet.

"Want company?" Dax offered. "Mireclaw and I have been meaning to check on the outer districts anyway."

"Thanks, but this is something I need to do alone."

The journey to her childhood home took less than an hour, but it felt like traveling between worlds. The outer districts of Calyss had always been quieter than the city center, places where families lived and worked without much involvement in the grand politics of the Council. Now they hummed with a different kind of energy—the productive chaos of people discovering new possibilities.

She passed a bakery where the owner's Guardian wheat-spirit was working alongside a newly manifested shadow-mouse to create bread that somehow managed to be both nutritious and incredibly flavorful. A blacksmith whose tools now carried both light and shadow was forging metal with a precision that would have been impossible under the old system. Children played in the streets with spirits that shifted fluidly between Guardian and demon aspects, treating the transformation like an exciting game rather than a cosmic upheaval.

Her parents' house looked exactly the same from the outside—a modest two-story building with a workshop attached, surrounded by the garden her mother had tended for as long as Kaela could remember. But something felt different as she approached the front door, something that made her pause with her hand raised to knock. The air in her old neighborhood now carried a faint, ozone-like tang, the scent of a world where the veil between spirits and mortals had worn thin.

The house felt... alive. Not empty or waiting, but actively inhabited by presences that welcomed her approach.

"Kaela?" Her mother's voice came from inside, followed by the sound of rapid footsteps. The door opened before she could announce herself, revealing a woman whose face showed every day of worry from the past four months.

But it was the spirit hovering behind her mother that made Kaela gasp in surprise.

"You're bonded," she said, staring at the delicate butterfly whose wings seemed to contain entire galaxies.

"Three days ago," her mother confirmed, stepping aside to let Kaela enter. "Right after the transformation. I was gardening when suddenly... she was there. Like she'd been waiting for me my entire life."

The house felt different inside, too. Brighter somehow, but also more peaceful. Her father's workshop tools, which she could see through the connecting doorway, glowed with subtle light that shifted between colors as she watched.

"Where's Father?" she asked.

"Here," came a familiar voice from the workshop. Her father emerged, looking older than she remembered but also somehow more solid, more present. Behind him floated a spirit that looked like a small dragon made of living metal and flame.

"Hello, daughter," he said simply, and the word carried none of the careful politeness she'd feared. Just love, uncomplicated and unconditional.

For a moment, they stood there looking at each other—three people who had shared a house for sixteen years but had never really seen each other clearly. Then her mother stepped forward and pulled her into a hug that smelled like soap and herbs and home.

"We're so sorry," her mother whispered. "For the exile, for the years of making you feel like you were broken, for believing the Council's lies about what you needed to become whole."

"You weren't the only ones who believed," Kaela said, hugging her back with careful control. The last thing she wanted was to accidentally incinerate her parents with Ignivane's enthusiasm. "The whole world believed. That's what made it so hard to fight."

"Tell us," her father said, settling into his favorite chair while his dragon-spirit curled around his shoulders like a living scarf. "Tell us what happened. All of it. We want to understand."

So Kaela told them everything. The exile, the Shadebond camp, the growing resistance, the discovery of the Council's lies, the desperate battles that had led to the transformation. She told them about Ember's sacrifice, about the fusion network's failure, about the moment when she'd realized that cooperation was stronger than control.

Her parents listened without interruption, their new spirits providing a running commentary of emotional reactions—amazement, horror, pride, grief, and finally, understanding.

"You saved the world," her mother said when the story was finished.

"We saved the world," Kaela corrected. "All of us, together. That was the whole point—no one person could have done this alone."

"But you started it," her father said. "You refused to accept that being whole was impossible."

"I was lucky enough to bond with someone who helped me figure that out," Kaela replied, feeling Ashfang's presence stir within Ignivane's consciousness. "And stubborn enough to keep trying even when it seemed hopeless."

They spent the afternoon talking about smaller things—how the transformation had affected the neighborhood, what changes were happening in her father's craft, how her mother's new bond was influencing her gardening. It was wonderfully, perfectly ordinary, the kind of family conversation she'd thought she'd lost forever.

But as the sun began to set, her father grew serious again.

"There's something else we need to discuss," he said. "The Council loyalists who fled the city. They're not gone—they're organizing in the Borderlands, trying to convince people that the transformation was a disaster that needs to be reversed."

"Reversed how?"

"We don't know. But they're claiming that Eidolon consciousness is unstable, that the unified spirits will eventually drive their hosts insane." His dragon-spirit flared with protective fire. "They're using fear to recruit people who are struggling with the changes."

Kaela felt a familiar weight settle on her shoulders. Of course it couldn't be that simple. Of course destroying the Great Seal wouldn't solve every problem or convert every opponent.

"How many?"

"Maybe a few hundred, concentrated around the old military outposts. Not enough to threaten the cities, but enough to cause problems for isolated communities."

"And they're led by?"

"Former Councilor Thorne, apparently. He survived the transformation but rejected his new bond. Now he's claiming that the old ways were better, that people were happier when they didn't have to deal with spiritual complexity."

Through Ignivane's consciousness, Kaela felt a mixture of responses. Ashfang's sardonic amusement at the idea that ignorance was bliss. Aurelia's fierce protectiveness toward the communities that might be threatened. And her own growing understanding that the revolution's work was far from over.

"We'll handle it," she said finally. "Not with overwhelming force—that would just prove their point about Eidolons being dangerous. But we'll find a way to demonstrate that cooperation works better than nostalgia."

"You don't have to handle it alone," her mother said gently. "That's what we learned from your story— that trying to carry everything by yourself is what leads to breaking."

"I know. And I won't." Kaela stood up, feeling the pull of responsibility but also the support of people who loved her. "But I should get back to the city. There are people depending on the provisional government to figure out how to make this work."

"Will you come back?" her father asked. "Not just for visits, but... will you consider this home again?"

Kaela looked around the house where she'd grown up—the same rooms, the same furniture, but transformed by the presence of spirits who had freely chosen to be there. It felt like home, but also like something larger than home. A place where she was loved for who she was rather than who she might become.

"Yes," she said. "When the work is done, when people don't need me to help hold things together anymore. I'll come home."

Her parents' smiles made the promise feel like a sacred oath.

As she walked back toward the city center, Kaela reflected on how much had changed in just four months. The scared, desperate girl who had called for any spirit that would have her was gone, replaced by someone who understood that strength came from connection rather than isolation.

The reckonings weren't finished—there would be more conversations like this one, more people who needed to face the truth of what the old system had cost them. But each conversation, each moment of understanding, each choice to embrace wholeness over division made the new world a little more stable.

Through Ignivane's consciousness, she felt the satisfaction of work well done and the anticipation of work yet to come. There were still Council loyalists to convince, still communities to help through their transformations, still institutions to build that would serve a world where cooperation was the norm rather than the exception.

The desperate girl who craved a single, perfect victory was gone. The woman she'd become understood that building a world required getting a thousand small things right, and she was finally ready to begin.

They'd broken the cycle of separation. Now they just had to prove that what they'd built to replace it was worth preserving.

Chapter 25: Shade Academy

The old Guardian training facility had been abandoned since the transformation, its pristine white walls and ceremonial dueling circles no longer serving any useful purpose. But as Kaela walked through the empty corridors with Dax and Captain Lyr, she could see its potential—not as a monument to the old ways, but as something entirely new.

"The bones are good," Captain Lyr observed, his wolf-stag Eidolon moving with the fluid grace that still caught people off guard. "Solid construction, excellent ventilation, practice spaces designed for spiritual work. We'd just need to... reimagine the purpose."

"From the Calyss Academy for Guardian Excellence to what?" Dax asked, running her hand along a wall where faded murals showed the traditional progression from Naming Day to graduation.

"The Academy for Integrated Consciousness," Kaela said, the name feeling right as soon as she spoke it. "A place where people can learn to work with their whole selves instead of fighting half of them."

It had been Ember's idea, originally—establishing formal training programs for the techniques they'd developed in the Shadebond camps. With the

217

transformation complete, there were thousands of people struggling to understand their new spiritual capabilities, and the informal support networks they'd built couldn't handle the demand.

"The curriculum would need to be completely different," Captain Lyr said, studying the layout of the practice halls. "The old Guardian training was all about discipline, control, suppression of anything that didn't fit the approved mold."

"And the new training?" Dax prompted.

"Cooperation," Kaela replied immediately. "Feel, name, channel, balance—but expanded beyond individual bonds to include working with others, understanding different types of spiritual integration, building communities that support wholeness rather than demanding conformity."

They spent the morning walking through the facility, taking notes on what could be salvaged and what needed to be completely rebuilt. The ceremonial chambers where Guardian spirits had been summoned would become spaces for meditation and self-reflection. The dueling circles would be converted into areas for cooperative exercises and group work. The library, filled with texts that preached separation and purity, would be restocked with materials that acknowledged the full spectrum of spiritual experience.

"The biggest challenge," Captain Lyr said as they reviewed their plans over lunch, "will be finding instructors who understand integration well enough to teach it safely."

"We've got maybe two dozen people with real expertise," Dax agreed. "Enough to train the first generation of students, but not enough to scale up quickly."

"Then we start small," Kaela said. "A pilot program with carefully selected students and instructors. Focus on developing the teaching methods before we worry about reaching everyone."

"And who teaches the teachers?" Captain Lyr asked. "Most of us learned these techniques through trial and error, often in life-or-death situations. That's not exactly a replicable educational model."

It was a fair point. The skills that had carried them through the revolution—the ability to form bonds across traditional boundaries, to work with shadow aspects instead of suppressing them, to find balance between opposing forces—had been learned through necessity and desperation. Turning that into a formal curriculum would require a completely different approach.

"We iterate," Kaela said finally. "Start with what we know works, test it with small groups, refine based on what we learn. The same way we developed the fusion techniques—through practice, feedback, and constant adjustment."

Their planning was interrupted by a commotion outside. Through the windows, they could see a crowd gathering in the academy's courtyard—not angry or threatening, but clearly agitated about something.

"What now?" Dax muttered, checking her weapons out of habit.

They found about fifty people clustered around a familiar figure: Councilor Thorne, his face seemed to have caved in on itself, the sharp lines of his conviction softened into a mask of weary bitterness, but speaking with the same authoritative voice that had once commanded respect in the Council chambers.

"—telling you that this transformation is not natural," he was saying to the assembled crowd. "The spirits were separated for good reason. Integration leads to madness, to the kind of chaos that destroys civilizations."

"Councilor Thorne," Kaela called, stepping into the courtyard with her companions flanking her. "I thought you'd left the city."

"I had. But reports of what you're planning here reached us in the Borderlands." He gestured at the academy building with obvious distaste. "A school for teaching people to embrace corruption? To celebrate the very spiritual contamination that the Council spent centuries trying to prevent?"

"A school for teaching people to be whole," Kaela corrected. "Something the Council never figured out how to do."

"Wholeness." Thorne's laugh was bitter. "Look around you, child. Look at the confusion, the instability, the people who can't handle the sudden rush of spiritual input. This is what your 'wholeness' has brought us."

He wasn't entirely wrong. The transformation had been traumatic for many people, and the adjustment period was proving longer and more difficult than anyone had anticipated. Some formerly Hollow individuals were struggling with sudden spiritual awareness. Some Guardian-bonded people couldn't adapt to having shadow aspects. And some demon-bonded people were overwhelmed by the addition of light elements to their consciousness.

"Change is hard," Kaela acknowledged. "But that doesn't mean it's wrong. The people who are struggling need support and education, not a return to the system that broke them in the first place."

"The system that kept them safe," Thorne countered. "The system that prevented the kind of spiritual chaos that nearly destroyed the world five centuries ago."

"The system that was built on lies," Captain Lyr interjected, his Eidolon nature making his voice carry unusual authority. "I served that system for twenty years, Councilor. I believed in it completely. But I've seen what cooperation can accomplish, and I won't go back to pretending that half of existence is evil."

"You've been corrupted by proximity to demon influences," Thorne said dismissively. "The same way all of you have been corrupted. You think you're making rational choices, but you're actually being manipulated by spiritual parasites that have convinced you their presence is beneficial."

Murmurs ran through the crowd—some supportive of Thorne's position, others clearly skeptical. These were people who had lived through the transformation, who had experienced integration firsthand. They knew the difference between manipulation and partnership.

"Demonstrate," Dax said suddenly.

"What?" Thorne looked confused.

"Demonstrate the corruption you're talking about. Show us how my partnership with Mireclaw has made me less rational, less capable, less human." Dax's poison-and-healing serpent manifested around her shoulders, its scales shifting through the full spectrum from venomous green to healing gold. "Explain how working with both death and life, poison and medicine, shadow and light has diminished me."

"Show us how my wolf-stag consciousness has made me a worse leader," Captain Lyr added. "How understanding both predatory instincts and protective care has compromised my judgment."

"Demonstrate how Ignivane's triple consciousness has reduced my ability to think clearly or make ethical choices," Kaela finished. "Prove that integration is corruption instead of just claiming it."

For a moment, Thorne looked like he might try to meet their challenge. But then his expression grew crafty, calculating.

"You want a demonstration? Very well." He raised his hands, and pale light began to gather around him—not the warm golden glow of healthy Guardian magic, but something cold and brittle. "I'll show you what happens when spiritual contamination is forcibly removed."

The attack came without warning—not physical violence, but a spiritual assault designed to sever their Eidolon bonds and return them to the separated state that Thorne considered natural. It was the same technique the Council had used in their "purification" chambers, weaponized and directed at people he considered irredeemably corrupt.

It might have worked, if they'd been operating as individuals.

But the crowd in the courtyard included dozens of people with various levels of integration—some full Eidolons, some partial fusions, some just beginning to explore their shadow aspects. And when Thorne's attack hit, they responded not with panic or resistance, but with instinctive cooperation.

Guardian and demon aspects flowed together throughout the crowd, creating a network of shared consciousness that absorbed and dissipated the severance magic like water soaking into sand. What should have been a devastating assault became nothing more than an unpleasant sensation, easily managed by people working together.

"That's how you demonstrate corruption?" asked one of the crowd—a baker whose bread-spirit had recently gained fascinating shadow properties. "By trying to hurt people who've done nothing to you?"

"By trying to force your choices on others?" added a mother whose young daughter had manifested Eidolon consciousness at age eight. "By deciding that your way is the only acceptable way?"

Thorne stared at the crowd, clearly expecting fear and submission but finding only disappointment and pity. His grand gesture had not only failed but had actually demonstrated the opposite of what he'd intended—that cooperation was stronger than coercion, that integration was more stable than separation.

Captain Lyr stepped forward, his Eidolon presence radiating not menace, but a calm and unshakable authority. "No, Thorne, it isn't over. But your part in it is." He wasn't speaking to the old Councilor, but to the crowd, his voice resonating with the full weight of the New Concordat. "Our new world is founded on choice and cooperation, not fear. We will not exile him. We will not imprison him. We will simply... move on."

He then looked directly at Thorne, his voice dropping but losing none of its power. "You are no longer a Councilor. You hold no authority here. You are just a man, free to live with the consequences of your choices, but never again to make them for others."

Thorne searched the crowd for any sign of support, for any flicker of the old fear he used to command, and found only pity and disinterest. His power wasn't defeated in a battle; it had simply evaporated. He turned and walked away, not a defiant leader in retreat, but a bitter, irrelevant old man, swallowed by the future he had refused to accept.

As he disappeared from view, the crowd's mood shifted from tense to celebratory.

People who had been worried about the confrontation were now discussing what they'd just experienced—the way their different types of integration had spontaneously coordinated, the sense of being part of something larger than themselves.

"Well," Captain Lyr said, "I think we just figured out our first curriculum module."

"Community defense?" Dax asked.

"Community cooperation," Kaela corrected. "How to work together instinctively, how to support each other's spiritual growth, how to build networks that strengthen everyone involved."

They spent the rest of the afternoon talking with the people who had spontaneously defended the academy, learning about their experiences with integration and their ideas for what the school should teach. By evening, they had the outline of a curriculum that was both practical and inspiring— focused on real skills that people needed, but grounded in principles of mutual support and voluntary cooperation.

"Module One: Consent and Safety," Kaela read from their notes as they wrapped up for the day. "Bond check-in phrases, stop words, posture, breathing techniques."

"Module Two: Emotion Naming," Dax continued. "Daily reflection journals, shadow sketching, understanding the full spectrum of feelings."

"Module Three: Channel Basics," Captain Lyr added. "Controlled manifestation, cooldown routines, recognizing and managing spiritual exhaustion."

The full eight-week program they'd outlined was ambitious but achievable—a structured path from basic safety to advanced cooperation techniques. And more importantly, it was something that could be replicated anywhere people were willing to learn.

"We'll need to document everything carefully," Kaela said as they locked up the academy for the night. "Not just what to teach, but how to teach it, how to adapt it for different types of integration, how to handle problems that come up."

"The 'How to Train Your Demon' manual?" Dax suggested with a grin.

"More like the 'How to Be Whole' guide," Kaela replied. "Though I admit your title has a better ring to it."

As they walked back toward the city center, Kaela felt a deep satisfaction settling in her chest. The Academy for Integrated Consciousness would be more than just a school—it would be proof that the new world they were building could sustain itself, could pass its values on to the next generation, could grow and adapt without losing its essential character.

The revolution had torn down the old system. Now they were building something better to replace it, one lesson at a time.

And judging by the enthusiasm they'd seen today, people were ready to learn.

Chapter 26: New Treaties

The negotiations began at dawn in the ruins of the old Council chamber, with representatives from seven different factions gathered around a table that had been hastily constructed from crystalline fragments and salvaged wood.

Kaela studied the faces across from her, marveling at how much the world had changed in just six weeks. Guardian-bonded traditionalists sat beside demon-bonded revolutionaries. Former Council loyalists shared space with Borderland refugees. Newly-manifested Eidolons worked alongside people who remained unbonded by choice. And scattered throughout were the ordinary citizens whose voices had been ignored for centuries but who now demanded a seat at the table where their future was being decided.

"The first order of business," announced Elder Vera, the de facto leader of the traditionalist faction, "is establishing clear boundaries for spiritual manifestation in public spaces."

"Boundaries?" Dax's voice carried a dangerous edge. "We just spent months fighting a war to eliminate artificial boundaries between spirits."

"Not elimination—regulation," Elder Vera clarified. "The transformation may have changed our spiritual capabilities, but it hasn't changed the need for public safety and social order."

Kaela felt Ignivane's triple consciousness stir with careful interest. This was exactly the kind of conflict they'd anticipated—people who accepted the new reality but wanted to control its expression, to make it safe and predictable and comfortable.

"What kind of regulation are you proposing?" asked Marcus Brightfield, speaking for the Borderland communities. His Guardian hawk-spirit had recently integrated with shadow aspects, making him uniquely positioned to bridge different perspectives.

"Designated areas for advanced spiritual work," Elder Vera replied, producing a scroll covered in detailed diagrams. "Public spaces where people can practice fusion techniques, private zones where Eidolon consciousness won't overwhelm those who prefer separation, certified instructors for anyone seeking to develop their capabilities."

"Spiritual segregation, you mean," Captain Lyr said flatly. "Put the 'dangerous' integrated people in their own areas where they won't upset the normals."

"Practical accommodation," Elder Vera corrected. "Not everyone is comfortable with the level of spiritual intensity that Eidolons naturally radiate. Some people need spaces where they can exist without constant reminders of capabilities they don't possess or don't want."

It was a reasonable concern, actually. The transformation had created an enormous range of spiritual states—from full Eidolon consciousness to partial integration to voluntary separation. Managing that diversity without creating new forms of discrimination was proving more complex than anyone had anticipated.

"Counter-proposal," said Lila Ashworth, representing the newly-bonded citizens. "Instead of segregation, we establish protocols. Guidelines for how to moderate spiritual presence in mixed company, training for people who want to work on integration, support networks for those who are struggling with the changes."

"And who enforces these protocols?" asked Jeremiah Cole, the representative for those who remained unbonded by choice. "Who decides what level of spiritual manifestation is acceptable in a given situation?"

The question hung in the air like a challenge. Because that was the core issue they were dancing around—not just what rules to make, but who would have the authority to make them. The old system had been simple: the Council decided everything, and everyone else complied or faced exile. But that hierarchy was gone, replaced by something messier and more democratic.

"Community standards," Kaela said finally. "Decisions made at the local level by the people who have to live with them. Some neighborhoods might want intensive spiritual integration. Others might prefer more conservative approaches. As long as no one is forced to conform to standards they didn't help create, people can organize themselves however they want."

"And what about disputes between communities?" Elder Vera asked. "What happens when integrated and non-integrated groups come into conflict?"

"The same thing that happens now when any groups come into conflict," Dax replied. "Negotiation, mediation, compromise. The tools for resolving disagreements peacefully already exist—we just need to apply them."

"But we also need mechanisms for handling situations where negotiation fails," Captain Lyr added. "Some kind of dispute resolution system that doesn't rely on hierarchical authority but can still maintain peace."

They spent the next three hours working through scenarios—what to do about Eidolons whose natural presence disrupted nearby spirits, how to handle people who used their enhanced capabilities to intimidate others, what rights unbonded citizens had in communities where spiritual integration was the norm.

Each discussion revealed new layers of complexity. The transformation hadn't just changed individual capabilities—it had fundamentally altered the social dynamics that governed how people related to each other. Old assumptions about power, authority, and community organization no longer applied.

"Break for lunch," Kaela announced when it became clear that they were starting to argue in circles. "We'll reconvene in two hours."

As the delegates scattered to find food and decompress, Kaela found herself walking through the city with Captain Lyr and Dax, trying to process what they'd learned from the morning's discussions.

"It's harder than I thought it would be," she admitted. "During the revolution, we were fighting for the right to exist as we are. But now we have to figure out how to exist as we are while still living alongside people who made different choices."

"The Council never had to worry about this," Captain Lyr observed. "They just declared one way right and every other way wrong. Much simpler from a governance perspective."

"And much more brutal from a human perspective," Dax added. "At least now people get to choose their own level of spiritual engagement instead of having it chosen for them."

They passed a small park where children were playing—some with visible spirit-bonds, others without, all of them apparently oblivious to the political complexities their parents were struggling with. A girl with a shadow-butterfly spirit was teaching an unbonded boy how to sense spiritual presences. A pair of Eidolon twins were sharing their enhanced perception with a group of traditionally-bonded children.

"They make it look easy," Kaela said, watching the casual cooperation.

"Because for them, it is easy," Captain Lyr replied. "They don't have years of conditioning telling them that different types of spiritual development are inherently incompatible."

"Which suggests that maybe our real challenge isn't figuring out how to manage diversity—it's figuring out how to support the adults while the children teach us what cooperation actually looks like."

The afternoon session was more productive, partly because everyone had eaten but mostly because they'd shifted from trying to solve everything at once to focusing on immediate, practical concerns.

"First priority," announced Elder Vera, "is emergency response protocols. What happens when someone's spiritual integration goes wrong and they need immediate intervention?"

"Second priority," added Marcus Brightfield, "is education and training standards. Not everyone needs formal instruction, but people who want it should know where to find qualified teachers."

"Third priority," said Lila Ashworth, "is economic integration. How do we handle people whose enhanced capabilities give them unfair advantages in traditional professions? Or people whose chosen level of integration limits their employment options?"

They made real progress on all three issues. Emergency response would be handled by teams that included both medical personnel and spiritual specialists, with protocols for different types of integration crises. Education would be managed through a network of certified academies, but with local control over curriculum and admission standards. Economic concerns would be addressed through new guild structures that accounted for enhanced capabilities while protecting traditional workers.

"The Treaty of Calyss," Captain Lyr said as they reviewed their agreements at the end of the day. "Has a nice ring to it."

"More like the Beginning of the Treaty of Calyss," Dax corrected. "We've covered maybe ten percent of the issues we're going to need to address."

She was right. They'd made a start on formal governance for the post-transformation world, but there were hundreds of details still to be worked out. Questions about trade between integrated and non-integrated communities. Protocols for handling people whose spiritual development posed genuine risks to others. Standards for the new academies that were springing up across the continent.

"But it's a good start," Kaela said, reading through the preliminary agreements they'd drafted. "And more importantly, it's a start that everyone can live with."

The key insight that had emerged from the negotiations was simple but profound: the new world didn't need to be uniform to be stable. Different communities could make different choices about spiritual integration as long as they respected each other's right to exist. The old Council had failed because it tried to impose one vision on everyone. The new system would succeed by supporting many visions, all coexisting peacefully.

"One more thing," Elder Vera said as they prepared to adjourn. "What do we call ourselves? What name do we give to this new form of government?"

The question sparked a brief debate. Republic? Federation? Alliance? Each term carried implications about structure and authority that didn't quite fit what they were building.

"The Confederation of Free Communities," suggested Marcus Brightfield. "Emphasis on voluntary association and local autonomy."

"The Integrated Commonwealth," countered Lila Ashworth. "Something that acknowledges our spiritual diversity while emphasizing shared purpose."

"The Cooperative Territories," offered Jeremiah Cole. "Neutral language that doesn't prioritize any particular form of spiritual development."

In the end, they settled on something elegantly simple: the New Concordat. An agreement to disagree peacefully, to support each other's choices while maintaining their own autonomy, to build a world where cooperation was voluntary rather than imposed.

As the delegates departed to take word of the agreements back to their communities, Kaela felt a deep satisfaction settling in her chest. Not the satisfaction of victory—this wasn't about winning and losing—but the satisfaction of building something that could last.

"Think it'll work?" Dax asked as they watched the last representatives disappear into the evening shadows.

"Ask me in ten years," Kaela replied. "But I think we've given it the best chance possible."

Through Ignivane's consciousness, she felt the truth of those words. They'd created a framework for peaceful coexistence, but frameworks were only as strong as the people who used them. The real test would come when communities faced their first serious conflicts, when the idealism of the early days ran up against the practical challenges of governing diverse populations.

But they'd proven that cooperation was possible, even between people who had very different ideas about how life should be lived. And if they could do it once, they could do it again.

The age of imposed unity was over. The age of chosen cooperation was just beginning.

Chapter 27: Rift Whispers

The first reports came from Borderland traders—
stories of strange lights dancing over the Abyssal
Rift, sounds that carried for miles despite having no
visible source, and animals behaving in ways that
suggested they could sense something humans
couldn't.

Kaela read through the collected testimonies in her
temporary office at the Academy, trying to parse
signal from noise. Many of the accounts were clearly
exaggerated—traders had a tendency toward
dramatic storytelling when it helped sell their goods.
But there were enough consistent details to suggest
something real was happening at the site of the
original Sundering.

"Auroral displays visible from fifty miles away," she
read aloud to Dax and Captain Lyr. "Music that
sounds like singing crystals. Ground tremors that
follow no geological pattern. And multiple reports of
Eidolon manifestations that appear and disappear
without any human bonded partners."

"Wild Eidolons?" Dax looked skeptical. "Spirits that
achieved integration without human involvement?"

"It's theoretically possible," Captain Lyr said
thoughtfully. "The transformation didn't just affect

bonded spirits—it healed the fundamental rift between light and shadow throughout the magical ecosystem. If separated spirits in the wild found each other..."

"Then we might be looking at the first natural Eidolon formations in five centuries," Kaela finished. "The question is whether that's cause for celebration or concern."

Through Ignivane's consciousness, she felt a complex mixture of emotions—Ashfang's curiosity about what might be awakening, Aurelia's protective instincts toward any spirits struggling with integration, and her own growing sense that their work was far from finished.

"There's something else," Captain Lyr said, producing a message crystal that flickered with unstable light. "This arrived from the Rift Watch station this morning. The automated monitoring systems we left there are detecting massive spiritual disturbances—energy levels comparable to what we saw during the Great Seal's final activation."

Kaela felt a chill run down her spine. The Rift Watch had been established to monitor the site where the original Sundering had torn reality apart, to ensure that healing the Great Seal hadn't caused any unexpected consequences. The fact that it was now detecting spiritual activity on the scale of their climactic battle was deeply troubling.

"Could it be aftershocks?" Dax asked. "Some kind of delayed reaction to breaking the Seal?"

"Or it could be something that was sleeping under the Rift finally waking up," Captain Lyr replied grimly. "The original Sundering didn't just split spirits—it wounded the fundamental structure of reality. We healed the surface damage, but if there were deeper injuries..."

He didn't need to finish the thought. They'd all seen what happened when spiritual forces of that magnitude were left uncontrolled. The Great Seal had been created to contain the damage from the first Sundering, but it had also been slowly poisoning the world for five centuries. If there were other wounds left by the original catastrophe, wounds that their healing had now exposed...

"We need to investigate," Kaela said, though the words felt like accepting a burden she'd hoped never to carry again. "Whatever's happening at the Rift, we can't ignore it."

"A small team," Dax suggested. "Fast, quiet, prepared for anything. If this is dangerous, we don't want to expose too many people to it."

"And if it's not dangerous but requires immediate action?"

"Then we send word back and organize a proper response. But we go in careful until we know what we're dealing with."

It was a sensible plan, but as Kaela looked around at the peaceful Academy grounds—students practicing integration exercises, instructors developing new teaching methods, the quiet work of building a better world—she felt a familiar reluctance to leave it all behind for another desperate mission into the unknown.

"I don't have to be the one who goes," she said finally. "There are other people qualified to handle this kind of investigation."

"Are there?" Captain Lyr asked gently. "People who understand both the historical context and the current spiritual landscape? People who've successfully worked with unstable magical phenomena on this scale?"

"People who've actually been inside the heart of a Great Seal ritual and lived to tell about it?" Dax added. "Because I'm pretty sure that's a very short list."

They were right, and Kaela knew it. Like it or not, her experiences during the revolution had given her a unique understanding of large-scale spiritual phenomena. And Ignivane's triple consciousness provided capabilities that might be essential for safely investigating whatever was happening at the Rift.

"Three days to organize the mission," she decided. "Small team, as Dax suggested. Essential personnel only, and everyone volunteers—no one gets volunteered for this."

"Who do we ask?" Captain Lyr inquired.

Kaela thought about it. They'd need someone with deep theoretical knowledge of spiritual mechanics, someone with healing capabilities in case things went wrong, someone with experience in hostile environments, and someone who could serve as a communication link back to the Academy.

"Scholar Wynne for theoretical expertise," she said finally. "Her crystal hart has been studying the transformation's effects on magical theory. Healer Santos for medical support—his storm-crane Eidolon has proven remarkably effective at stabilizing traumatic spiritual injuries. And..."

She paused, considering. The team needed to be small enough to move quickly but large enough to handle unexpected complications. Too many people would be unwieldy; too few would be vulnerable.

"Maya Thornfield," Dax suggested. "Her shadow-wolf partnership has been doing reconnaissance work in the Borderlands. She knows the terrain around the Rift better than anyone."

"And Tam Brightwater," Captain Lyr added. "If we need to send messages back quickly, his wind-spirit bond is the fastest communication method we have."

It was a good team—diverse capabilities, proven under pressure, small enough to avoid drawing unwanted attention. But as Kaela thought about leading them into whatever was stirring at the Abyssal Rift, she felt the weight of responsibility settling around her shoulders like an old, familiar cloak.

"There's one more thing," she said. "If this turns out to be connected to the original Sundering—if we're dealing with some kind of ancient magical disaster that we accidentally triggered—then we might be looking at threats that make the Great Seal seem simple by comparison."

"Meaning?" Dax asked.

"Meaning this could be the beginning of a much larger challenge. Something that requires resources and cooperation on a scale we've never attempted." Kaela looked out the window toward the city, where people were still learning how to live with their transformed reality. "We've barely figured out how to govern ourselves peacefully. Are we ready to handle cosmic-level magical crises?"

"Probably not," Captain Lyr admitted. "But that's never stopped us before."

"And besides," Dax added with a grin that was only slightly forced, "what's the worst that could happen? Another ancient magical disaster threatens to destroy the world, and we have to figure out how to stop it with improvised cooperation and stubborn determination?"

"Don't tempt fate," Kaela warned, but she found herself smiling despite her concerns.

The next three days passed in a blur of preparation and planning. Supplies for a week-long expedition into dangerous territory. Coordination with the Borderland communities who would need to be warned if something went wrong. Messages to other major cities explaining the situation and requesting support if needed.

But most importantly, conversations with the people who would be staying behind—reassurances that the Academy would continue functioning, that the New Concordat would be maintained, that the work of building a better world wouldn't stop just because its founders were away on another impossible mission.

"Try not to break anything else while we're gone," Captain Lyr advised the Academy's deputy director.

"Try not to find anything that needs breaking," she replied with a worried smile.

As the investigation team assembled at dawn on the fourth day, Kaela felt a familiar mixture of anticipation and dread. Not because she expected the mission to be dangerous—though it probably would be—but because she recognized the pattern. Just when things seemed stable, just when they'd built something worth preserving, the universe seemed to find new ways to test their resolve.

"Ready?" Dax asked, shouldering her pack with the easy grace of someone who'd spent months living rough in the Wilds.

"As ready as anyone can be for investigating mysterious disturbances at the site of a reality-warping magical catastrophe," Kaela replied.

"That's the spirit," Scholar Wynne said dryly. "Nothing builds confidence like acknowledging the impossibility of proper preparation."

As they set out toward the Abyssal Rift, following paths that had been dangerous even before the transformation, Kaela found herself thinking about cycles—how problems solved seemed to reveal new problems, how each victory enabled the next challenge, how the work of building a better world was never really finished.

But she also thought about growth—how each challenge they faced made them more capable of handling the next one, how their understanding of cooperation and integration had deepened with every crisis they'd survived together.

Whatever was stirring at the Rift, whatever ancient forces their healing of the Great Seal had awakened, they would face it the same way they'd faced everything else: together, with determination, and with the hard-won knowledge that separation was always weaker than unity.

The horizon beckoned with promise and threat in equal measure.

Chapter 28: Road Ahead

The Abyssal Rift stretched before them like a scar across the world's face, but as Kaela stood at the edge of the great chasm, she realized it no longer looked like a wound. The very ground seems to hum with a low, resonant frequency, like a sleeping giant.

The transformation had healed more than just individual spirits—it had begun healing the fundamental damage done to reality itself five centuries ago. Where once there had been jagged stone and twisted metal, where the very air had seemed to recoil from the violence of the original Sundering, now there was something that looked almost... alive.

"It's beautiful," Scholar Wynne breathed, her crystal hart spirit materializing beside her to better sense the magical currents that flowed through the canyon. "The theoretical models suggested this might happen, but seeing it..."

"Seeing it makes you realize the models didn't go nearly far enough," Healer Santos finished, his storm-crane Eidolon spreading wings that caught and reflected the strange aurora that danced above the Rift.

The lights were what had drawn them here—pillars of color that spiraled up from the canyon depths, painting the sky in shades that had no names. But up close, Kaela could see they weren't just lights. They were consciousness made visible, the dreams of spirits who were learning to be whole after centuries of enforced separation.

"There," Maya Thornfield pointed toward the canyon's eastern wall, where her shadow-wolf's enhanced senses had detected movement. "Something's moving down there. Something big."

Kaela followed her gaze and felt her breath catch. Emerging from what had once been a cave system carved by magical catastrophe was a figure that belonged in legends—an Eidolon the size of a building, with aspects of dragon and phoenix, storm and flame, earth and sky all flowing together in perfect harmony.

"Terragorn," Scholar Wynne whispered, consulting the ancient texts she'd brought. "Or something like him. One of the original Eidolons that was split during the Sundering."

"He's not hostile," Tam Brightwater reported, his wind-spirit bond allowing him to sense emotional currents from a distance. "Curious, maybe. Cautious. But not aggressive."

As if responding to their presence, the massive Eidolon turned toward them and spoke—not with a voice, but with a resonance that every bonded person present felt in their souls.

Welcome, children of healing. We have been waiting.

Through Ignivane's consciousness, Kaela felt the weight of centuries in those words. Not accusation or anger, but patient hope. The hope of beings who had been broken apart and scattered, who had endured separation and pain, who had finally been made whole again by the actions of people brave enough to choose cooperation over control.

"Waiting for what?" she asked, stepping closer to the Rift's edge.

For the next chapter to begin. For the children who healed the Great Wound to discover what lies beyond healing.

The massive spirit gestured with a wing that seemed to contain entire weather systems, indicating the depths of the canyon where more lights were beginning to emerge.

The Sundering did not just split spirits, young ones. It split the connections between worlds, between dimensions of existence that were meant to flow together. Your healing of the surface damage has begun to restore those connections.

"Other worlds?" Scholar Wynne's academic excitement was palpable. "You're talking about parallel dimensions? Alternate realities?"

We are talking about the full spectrum of existence, not just the narrow band that your people have called reality for five centuries. Places where different choices were made, where the Sundering never happened, where spirits evolved along paths your world has forgotten.

"And they're... opening up?" Healer Santos asked, his medical instincts clearly concerned about the implications of multidimensional rifts.

They are remembering how to touch each other. As spirits remember how to be whole, the barriers between world-layers grow thin. What you see as lights dancing in the sky are the dreams of other realities, bleeding through the healed spaces.

Kaela felt a mixture of awe and trepidation. They'd thought their work was finished—that healing the Great Seal and establishing the New Concordat would create the stable, peaceful world they'd been fighting for. But it seemed that was just the beginning.

"Is it dangerous?" she asked.

All growth is dangerous. All healing requires courage. But the alternative—remaining forever cut off from the full spectrum of existence—is a kind of death. The Eidolon's attention focused on her with an intensity that was both gentle and overwhelming. *You understand this, Kaela Veyne. You who chose wholeness over safety, integration over purity, love over control.*

Their unity was a constant dialogue in her soul: Ashfang's skepticism provided the anchor of stone and shadow, while Aurelia's vigilance was the soaring wind that missed no threat, but also something new—a sense of anticipation that belonged to all three of them. They'd spent so long fighting for the right to exist as they were that they'd never really considered what they might become if given the chance to grow.

"What do you need from us?" Captain Lyr asked, his wolf-stag nature allowing him to communicate with the ancient Eidolon on a level that pure humans couldn't match.

Nothing. Everything. What you have always given— the willingness to choose cooperation when separation would be easier, to build bridges when others would build walls, to trust in wholeness when the world demands division.

The massive spirit began to fade back into the canyon depths, but its voice continued to resonate in their consciousness.

The Academy you have built, the Concordat you have negotiated, the healing you have accomplished— these are the foundations for what comes next. Other worlds will send their own ambassadors, their own seekers, their own refugees from realities where the Sundering was never healed. You will need to teach them what you have learned, just as you will need to learn from what they have discovered.

"A multidimensional academy," Scholar Wynne said wonderfully. "A place where beings from different realities can learn to work together."

And more than that. A home for those who have nowhere else to go. A sanctuary for spirits seeking integration. A laboratory for discovering what cooperation looks like when the possibilities are truly infinite.

As the Eidolon's presence faded entirely, leaving only the dancing lights and the sense of vast potential stirring in the depths, Kaela found herself thinking about cycles again. Not the circular repetition of the same challenges, but the spiral growth that came from applying hard-won wisdom to ever-expanding possibilities.

"So," Dax said, her voice cutting through the contemplative silence, "I guess we're not retiring to quiet lives of teaching and governance after all."

"Were you planning to?" Maya asked with a grin.

"For about five minutes. But then I remembered that quiet lives are boring, and we're apparently constitutionally incapable of avoiding interesting disasters."

Kaela laughed, feeling the truth of that observation. They could have stayed in Calyss, could have focused on consolidating their gains and building stable institutions within the reality they knew. But that had never really been an option, had it? They were explorers by nature, bridge-builders, people who looked at barriers and saw opportunities for connection.

"Tam," she said, turning to their communications specialist, "send word back to the Academy. Tell them we've found the source of the disturbances, and it's not a threat—it's an invitation."

"An invitation to what?" he asked, already preparing his wind-spirit for the long journey back to civilization.

"To grow. To learn. To discover what happens when you take the principles of cooperation and integration and apply them to the entire multiverse."

As they made camp at the Rift's edge, preparing for a longer stay while they studied the phenomena and established proper contact protocols, Kaela felt something she hadn't experienced in months: the thrill of standing at the beginning of a great adventure.

The revolution was over. The old system of separation and control had been dismantled, replaced by something based on choice and cooperation. The immediate crises had been resolved, the emergency institutions had been established, the foundation for a better world had been laid.

But the work—the real work of building connections, of fostering understanding, of proving that love was stronger than fear—that work was just beginning. And now it would happen on a scale they'd never imagined, with teachers and students drawn from realities they were only beginning to glimpse.

"You know," Ashfang said through their bond as the sun set over the transformed Rift, painting the sky in colors that definitely didn't belong to their dimension, "when I answered your call at that Naming Day ceremony, I thought I was signing up for a simple bond with a desperate teenager."

"And instead?" Kaela asked, settling into her bedroll while Ignivane's triple consciousness kept watch for dimensional anomalies.

"Instead I got to help save the world, overthrow a theocracy, heal a five-hundred-year-old magical catastrophe, and apparently open the door to multidimensional cooperation between parallel realities." His mental voice carried familiar notes of sardonic amusement. "I have to admit, it's been more interesting than I expected."

"You think this was hard?" Aurelia added, her wind-spirit nature allowing her to sense the currents of possibility that flowed between worlds. "Wait for what's next."

Kaela smiled, looking up at stars that seemed to be shifting between familiar constellations and patterns that belonged to entirely different skies. The old Kaela—the one who'd stood in that silver circle four months ago, desperate to matter, terrified of being ordinary—would have been overwhelmed by the scope of what lay ahead.

But she wasn't that girl anymore. She was someone who'd learned that extraordinary didn't mean perfect, that strength came from connection rather than control, that the most important battles were fought not with overwhelming force but with patient love.

"Then we train harder," she said, echoing words Ashfang had spoken to her in what felt like a lifetime ago. "We learn faster. We build better bridges and stronger foundations and more inclusive communities."

"Together," Dax said from her own bedroll, Mireclaw coiled protectively around her shoulders.

"Together," Captain Lyr agreed, his wolf-stag spirit standing guard at the camp's perimeter.

"Together," the others chorused, their spirits adding their own notes of harmony to the pledge.

As Kaela drifted off to sleep, lulled by the gentle songs of interdimensional aurora and the steady presence of chosen family, she felt something she'd been searching for her entire life without knowing it: the absolute certainty that she was exactly where she belonged, doing exactly what she was meant to do, with exactly the right people by her side.

The road ahead stretched into possibilities she couldn't yet imagine, filled with challenges she wasn't yet prepared for, leading toward discoveries that would reshape everything they thought they knew about existence itself.

She couldn't wait to get started.

The horizon beckons toward the Abyssal Rift, where the original crime split spirits. Book 1 closes with hope—and the promise of larger forces awakening.

Epilogue: The Broken Chain

Six months after the Great Seal shattered, Kaela stood in the transformed Abyssal Rift watching something that shouldn't have been possible.

The scar that had marked the world for five centuries was healing itself. Where once there had been jagged stone and twisted metal, crystalline formations now grew in spiraling patterns that seemed to pulse with their own inner light. And moving between them, creatures of impossible beauty danced on currents of pure magic.

"The dimensional barriers are thinning," Scholar Wynne reported, consulting instruments that registered energies beyond normal human perception. "The healing process isn't just affecting our reality—it's opening pathways to others."

"Other worlds," Kaela mused, watching a butterfly the size of her hand phase in and out of visibility. Its wings seemed to contain entire galaxies, and when it looked at her, she felt the weight of vast, alien intelligence.

"Parallel realities where the Sundering never happened," Dax added, her own bond with Mireclaw having evolved into something that included aspects of both poison and pure healing. "Places where

Eidolons developed naturally, where cooperation was never seen as a threat."

Through Ignivane's consciousness—the triple merger of herself, Ashfang, and Aurelia that had become as natural as breathing—Kaela sensed movement in the deeper reaches of the Rift. Something vast stirring, something that had been waiting for the barriers to weaken enough to make contact.

"They're coming," she said, not sure if she meant it as warning or promise. "Whoever lives in those other realities, they know what we've done here. They're going to want to meet us."

"Ambassadors?" Captain Lyr suggested. His own transformation into a wolf-stag Eidolon had made him uniquely suited to diplomatic work, able to communicate with beings that existed on multiple levels of reality simultaneously.

"Or refugees," Scholar Wynne countered. "If there are realities where things went worse than they did here, where the forces of separation won completely..."

"Then we'll help them," Kaela said firmly. "The same way we helped each other. One person at a time, one choice at a time, one bridge at a time."

A new sound echoed across the Rift—not quite music, not quite language, but something that spoke directly to the part of the mind that understood connection. In the distance, shapes were moving among the crystalline formations. Tall, graceful figures that seemed to be made of solidified starlight, approaching with the careful caution of first contact.

"Well," Ashfang said through their bond, his mental voice carrying the familiar notes of sardonic amusement, "I have to admit, when I answered your call at that Naming Day ceremony, I never expected it to lead to interdimensional diplomacy."

"Think of it as the ultimate training exercise," Kaela replied, watching the starlight beings draw closer. "How to train your demon has apparently become how to train your multiverse."

The Academy they'd built, the Concordat they'd negotiated, the network of healers and teachers and bridge-builders they'd established—all of it had been preparation for this moment. The moment when their small revolution would expand beyond the boundaries of their world, when the principles of cooperation and integration would be tested on a scale they'd never imagined.

"Are you ready?" Dax asked, though the question was clearly rhetorical. None of them were ready for what was coming. How could anyone be ready for something that had never happened before?

"As ready as we can be," Kaela said, fire and shadow and wind dancing around her in patterns that would have been impossible before the transformation. "After all, we've already proven that impossible things are just things that haven't been done yet."

The starlight beings reached the edge of their camp, and Kaela stepped forward to meet them. Behind her, she could feel the presence of her chosen family—Dax and her poison-healer serpent, Captain Lyr and his wolf-stag wisdom, all the others who'd fought beside her to break the chains that held the world apart.

Ahead of her lay possibilities she couldn't even begin to comprehend. New worlds, new forms of consciousness, new challenges that would test everything they'd learned about building bridges between different kinds of existence.

But she'd learned something important over the past year: the work of connection was never finished. There would always be another wall to tear down, another boundary to cross, another impossible thing to make possible.

The difference was, now she knew she didn't have to do it alone.

"Welcome," she said to the beings of light, in words that somehow carried meaning despite the lack of shared language. "We've been waiting for you."

Through Ignivane's consciousness, she felt their response—curiosity, hope, recognition of kindred spirits who understood that separation was death and unity was life.

The next chapter of their story was about to begin. And this time, it would be written in the language of stars.

End of Book One

To be continued in:

*"Demon Trainer: **How to Bridge the Void**"...*

About the Authors

Ken Konet, M.Ed., MBA
By day, Ken Konet builds worlds — both in classrooms and across galaxies. A master of education and double MBA, Ken blends the precision of an engineer with the curiosity of a philosopher and the wild imagination of someone who clearly doesn't get enough sleep. When he isn't summoning demons onto the page or designing his next literary universe, he's chasing real-world horizons — hiking deep trails, camping under starlight, and carving along open roads on his motorcycle with his wife, Izzy, his constant companion in both mischief and motion.

Ken writes like a scientist who stole a poet's pen: analytical, funny, and occasionally explosive. If you ever meet him, bring coffee and a good argument — he collects both.

Ibrahim Roble
Ibrahim Roble is a Kenyan storyteller forged at the intersection of intellect and instinct — part philosopher, part chaos engineer. His work dismantles assumptions, rewires morality, and makes readers laugh in the very moment they're

questioning the universe. Ibrahim has an uncanny gift for giving voice to monsters, finding the heart in the dark, and making the impossible sound logical.

When collaborating with Ken, their process is less "writing session" and more "magical combustion." Together, they turn late-night brainstorms into epic sagas that balance danger, wit, and a touch of defiance toward anything resembling authority.

Together, they are equal parts fire and shadow — two creative forces writing at the speed of imagination. *Demon Trainer* is their shared act of rebellion against the ordinary: proof that the right partnership can make chaos coherent, and turn even a demon's story into a reflection of our own.

Other Books

Discover the many other works by these same authors:

- **Winnie the Pooh and the Vampire: A Very Bitey Problem**
- **Winnie the Pooh and The Zombies: A Rather Moaning Apocalypse**
- **Lucifera: The Anomaly**
- **The Meaning of YOUR Life: Build a Life That Matters-At Any Age, Any Stage**
- **Move Forward: Building Healthy Habits for a Fulfilling Life**
- **Stop Stepping on Rakes: Laugh at Your Mistakes, Learn from Them, and Keep Moving Forward**
- **The Engaged Leader: How to Build Trust, Empower Teams, and Lead with Impact**